It is only with the heart that one can see rightly; what is essential is invisible to the eye.

—Antoine de Saint-Exupéry,

Le Petit Prince

To have faith is to have wings.

—Peter Pan

RETURN TO THE CHILDREN'S HORRIBLE HOUSE

N. JANE QUACKENBUSH

For information regarding permission, write to:
Attention: Hidden Wolf Books
155 West Genung St., St. Augustine, FL 32086

Published in the United States by Hidden Wolf Books.

ISBN 9780996892209

Text set in Adobe Garamond
Designed by Philip Benjamin

Version 1.1
Printed in the United States of America
First edition hardcover printed, June 2018

To my family: Mom, Dad, Jeffrey, David, Jennifer, and Debbie. To my childhood inspirational friends Rebecca Burkley, Jennifer Price, Kendra Cabral. Kika Iadanza, for being a hawk-eye, laser beam proof-reader. My friendly supporters who encourage me in many ways to be better: Kristen Hendry, Martha DeForest, Catherine Maguire, Sol Felix, Kenia Warner, Christina Benjamin. My editor Beth Mansbridge and my graphic-designer Philip Benjamin.

The Children's Horrible House

The chil - dren's hor - i - ble house--

The chil - dren's hor - i - ble house--

Where you work all day------

And nev - er nev - er play----

The chil - dren's hor - i - ble house!

So … as you know, this is the song that literally came true.
I didn't believe my brothers and sisters
when they sang it to me.
You probably still don't believe it, do you?
Well, all I have to say is … I now know how to make
my bed and clean my room, and
you will too—if you know what's good for you …

HI, IT'S ME AGAIN, HOLLY.

CHAPTER 1

THAT REALLY DUMB DOG

"Hey, Mom?"

"Yes, Holly?"

"What's your favorite flower?"

"Hmm … I don't know. I'll have to think about it. … What's your favorite?"

"Passionflower," I said in my husky, just-out-of-bed voice.

I had woken from what seemed like the longest dream of my life. Like it lasted for months—not simply the all-nighter I had more usually. This dream had felt so real. I was taken to this amazing mansion that was so scary and spooky, yet marvelous and wondrous. A chill traveled through my spine as I replayed some of the details of my dream in my mind. I recalled being scared when I was alone in the gigantic mansion—especially on my exploring walks to THE DUNGEON. But as I thought it over, the haunted house was more than magnificent. It was beyond magical, and I decided I had a great dream and looked forward to having it again.

As I daydreamed while standing at the kitchen counter, my hand casually plunged deep inside my pocket. Within it I could feel something soft and fragile. It felt sort of like a wet tissue, but less snotty and boogery. Wait a second … it felt familiar. Could it be what it felt like? It couldn't be! I second-guessed myself … it had more of a velvety texture than a booger-filled snot rag. My fingers gently enveloped the rounded form within my pocket and pulled it out.

When my fingers unfolded, revealing the object in my palm, I couldn't believe my eyes. It wasn't an old tissue after all. Displayed within my palm, in all its colorful, soft-spiny fullness, lay the purple-faced passionflower I had found within the glowing garden back at The Children's Horrible House. I instantly thought about my dream and the moment when I had come face to face with this flower. Wait! Maybe it wasn't a dream. Could that haunted, breathing mansion be real? Did I really go there? My brain almost went blank as it tried to fathom the possibility of that place being real. I tried to figure out another place I could have found a passionflower bloom to put in my pocket. I couldn't think of any other possibility except that The Children's Horrible House actually existed and the whole experience I dreamed was real! A feeling of awe came over me as the reality of what I had barely survived flooded my consciousness.

Apparently, my stomach had something to say too; it gurgled its declarations of hunger. My brain filled with exhilarating images, but my mouth tasted … boring. My taste buds and stomach craved something exciting … like eggnog or even better, hot cocoa. I grabbed a pot, filled it with milk, placed it on the burner, and waited for it to get hot.

"Oh, yes … aren't they gorgeous?" my mom said after a long pause, as she prepared lasagna for our dinner guests. "They are more difficult to grow here in our climate. It's a bit too cold." She was responding as if I'd currently posed the question I'd asked her several moments ago. It had been so long I almost forgot what we were talking about. Sometimes my mom became lost in her own thoughts. I could tell because her face filled with silent expressions; eventually, she answered me.

"You mean they don't grow just anywhere?" I was puzzled as I stared at the wilting flower while waiting for my sweet treat to heat.

"Grow what? Where?" My dad walked in and gently punched the countertop, announcing his presence.

"Passionflowers, dear," my mother quickly answered.

"Passion what?" My dad's face crinkled to concerned bafflement. He looked over at me and my mom, wondering why we were talking about such questionable and uninteresting subjects. *He* preferred to talk about dinnertime, the other times when he would be fed, like breakfast and lunch—and cars.

I mixed in the cocoa and blew on it before taking a sip. *YUM* .... It tasted like Disney World. Disney was the first place I could remember having hot cocoa and whenever I had some, it brought me back to a sidewalk café where we watched the electric-light parade on Main Street and fireworks bursting over Cinderella's Castle.

"When will dinner be ready, dear?" This was a question my dad asked daily and the answer was always the same because he had set the time long before I was ever born to be six o'clock. I think he wanted to make sure everyone knew that dinnertime was not negotiable.

"Six o'clock, dear." My mother had a way of floating her voice out of a smiling mouth.

"Oh, good!" My dad smiled.

I slid off the barstool when I realized the conversation I'd been having with my mother was now over. I took my cocoa to the front porch and sat in the long wooden swing, with my feet dangling, barely long enough to give me a little push. I watched chirping birds flit from branch to branch while squirrels chased each other through the canopy of tall trees.

As I was swinging and enjoying my hot chocolate, my sister Ginger ran into the driveway toward the house, with her makeup running down her face. Her eyes looked like they were filled with overflowing black mud. The thick streaks that covered her cheeks made me giggle because she looked funny.

However, my laughter came to an abrupt halt when she screamed at me, "Filbert is gone! Is that funny? He ran away. I tried to … catch … him, but …."

I set my Goofy mug on the nearby table and followed my sister inside. This was serious—Ginger never cried. Her face showed the complete opposite expression of the normal glamorous model pout she normally wore.

"Good! He's a really dumb dog," Hickory, my oldest brother, heartlessly proclaimed as he bobbed his way around the foyer.

"How dare … how could you say such …" Ginger crumpled onto the oriental carpet.

My focus shifted to outside. Ginger's boyfriend, Basil, and his black sports car fishtailed into the driveway. My eyes widened with his impressive power slide. Basil jumped out of the T-top and ran to comfort Ginger. I glanced over at Hickory, who acted aloof to this entire situation. Hickory let out a quack-sounding fart that caused me to expel a humorous burst of air from my lips: "Phhhhhht!" I pretended to act disgusted, when normally *any* fart caused me to fall over in hysterics. But not now. That fart was not funny … okay, maybe a little funny. Actually, it was a lot funny, but I was too afraid of Ginger to giggle at the moment. I grabbed my long bunny ears and hid my sne

"Who let that duck in here?" Hickory looked at me with bright eyes and a wide smile, waiting for me to laugh … but I couldn't. After I successfully hid my smile, he snickered and made his usual *errrrrrrrrrrrrring* noises as he sauntered away farting some more. Hickory evidently was not the right sibling to look to for sympathy.

You know how when you're not supposed to laugh and then if you do laugh, you can't stop? I tried so hard to fight off my laughter that I had to pretend to be upset over Filbert to stop the giggles from taking over. I had to escape or find the right course of action in how to deal with the current situation.

Thankfully I gained control over myself. As my hands fell into my pocket, I felt my passionflower and thought about Coriander, Staniel, Danley, and Clover, my friends from The Children's Horrible House. If that place was real, then they were all real. Clover and I made a plan to introduce our dogs to one another. If I never found Filbert, how could we have a puppy playdate like we had talked about? There would be no special reason for us to get together. As much as I couldn't stand Filbert, I put those feelings aside and kneeled beside my sister's deflated form and promised her, "I will find him, Ginger … I will find Filbert."

CHAPTER 2

PROMISES

Ginger turned her black-smeared cheeks to me as snot dripped from her nose. She quickly panted in and out randomly as I tried especially hard to not burst out in laughter at her crinkled face and Hickory's earlier farts which now replayed in my head. "*Quack*" Guess I'm a bad person to come to when you're sad, too. Her eyes constricted as she read my face.

"I bet you're happy he's gone!" she roared. "You always hated him. And look, you're smiling … you probably made him run away!"

"No, no … it was Hickory's fart," I said, trying to make things better. "I mean, your face …"

She seemed even more shocked. "What about my face?"

"It looks … umm …" What was I saying?

"What?" she demanded.

"Umm, it looks funny, but … I will help find Filbert. I promise I will." I turned and scuttled away from the impact zone. Right now, Ginger was looking for someone to blame and I knew I would be her number one target.

I ran upstairs, racking my brain as to how I could find that dumb dog. In some ways, I didn't want to find him. He was a bothersome, blistering bunghole. Still, knowing Filbert could be the only link I had to Clover made me resolve to find him. My bunny ears bounced as I skipped through the upstairs hallway. I noticed Cashew busy doing what I thought was homework at his desk in his room. I detoured my course into his room and plopped onto his bed, right next to his desk.

"Did you hear about Filbert?" I asked.

In a dramatic voice, Cashew asked, "Is he dead?"

"No. He's run away."

"Are you sure?" he asked, still in a strange voice.

What was going on? Why was Cashew being so theatrical? Then I asked myself, *Am I sure Filbert is alive*? The answer was *No, I'm not sure*. However, I couldn't imagine Filbert dead. I somehow became sad and scared for the mutt.

Cashew let out a maniacal, "*MOO-HOO-huh-huh-haaah*! He's alive! He's alive!"

"Of course he is," I said.

Cashew lowered his head down to his desk like he was in some sort of fit, and began to growl.

"Why are you acting like this, Cashew?" I asked.

"Like what?" he asked in a scary voice.

"STOP!" I yelled, and quickly Cashew's expression changed into his normal, sweet, reassuring smile.

"It's okay, Holly. I'm merely practicing my lines for the Halloween play. I have to get in touch with my darker side in order pull off the role of Dr. Frankenstein." He reached out and gave my hat a pat.

"Oh … Filbert is missing and we have to find him."

He didn't exactly jump into action. In fact, he didn't move a muscle. He was staring at nothing … maybe he was practicing being still.

"Cashew?"

He blinked and came to.

"He's probably pooping everywhere … as usual … He'll be back to come and poop again eventually," he said nonchalantly.

"I think it's different this time. I've never seen Ginger so upset before. You should see her face." A little giggle snuck out as I remembered her black-smeared, ghoulish face.

"You seem really upset." Cashew's eyebrows tilted in sarcasm.

"I'm not, but I promised Ginger I would help her."

"So help her."

"I don't know what to do."

"I don't either."

"Can't you think of anything?"

He breathed out and said, "Why don't you make some fliers or call the pound? Put an ad in the paper in the lost-and-found section."

Why didn't I think of those things? Those ideas always worked on television. I jumped off Cashew's bed, ready to get to work—when the doorbell rang.

CHAPTER 3
THE FANGED FIEND

"Hey! I know you," the strange girl said to me. I could swear I did not know her. I had never seen her in all my life. I smiled 'cause she was smiling and I didn't want to make her feel bad.

"Don't you remember me?"

I guess my attempt to look convincing was not believable to this girl.

"Holly," my mom said, stepping in, "this is Camellia. The two of you went to nursery school together a few years ago. Don't you remember?"

Nursery school? Who remembers nursery school? I certainly didn't remember *this* Camellia from nursery school. And this was not the same Camellia from The Children's Horrible House who said *she knew me*. What was it with all these Camellia's and them knowing me?

I started to shake my head, when Camellia snuck over and took me by the arm and said, "Remember this?" She twisted my arm back and forth, giving me what everyone called an "Indian burn".

"Ouch!" I pulled my arm away.

When she smiled, I recognized the gnarled, cragged teeth she used to bite me with at nursery school—only bigger now, and more menacing. I pulled away even more.

"Camellia, is that nice?"

Her parents scolded much too leniently. She ignored them, letting herself inside my house. I looked up at my mom, hoping she'd send these jerks away. Instead, she invited them in!

"Happy birthday, Holly!" Camellia's mom handed me a gift.

I looked up at my mom. I'd forgotten that my birthday was so soon.

"I know it's a day early, but we decided to invite the Seedlings over for your birthday party," my mom said as if this should make me happy.

"Surprise!" Camellia said.

I was indeed surprised, but not in a good way.

The adults talked about the same old boring stuff all adults talk about, and if Camellia had been even a tiny bit interesting, I would have invited her to my room so we could play. I decided I should get to work on those missing posters for Filbert, so I snuck out of the kitchen.

This was not the birthday celebration I wanted, so I decided to pretend it was not really happening. I headed for my room when I saw Ginger lying on her bed, deep in thought, looking at her ceiling. She seemed sad and I felt bad for her. I stood in the doorway, trying to gauge if I should try to comfort her. I decided to go for it.

"Hi, Ginger. Is there anything I can do for you?"

"Get me some water," she said robotically.

I quickly turned and hopped downstairs. I took this task extremely seriously. I would be able to comfort my sister with this glass of water and she would be very grateful. I imagined her confiding in me, sharing her deepest thoughts, and we would bond together due to this token glass of water that could heal and cement our sisterhood. She hurt and I would be able to mend her sadness. She thirsted and I would be able to quench her yearning.

I picked a clean (this was very important), big, red, crackled-glass that used to be my grandmother's. I filled it with four ice cubes and then poured in filtered water. The vessel was filled with just the right amount of ice-to-water ratio, not overwhelmed with ice, rendering the water too chilly and not too warm, without enough ice. It held the perfect temperature required for optimal refreshment.

Gentle taps of ice cubes danced around in the glass as I climbed the stairs, being careful not to spill a drop. I proudly handed the chalice to Ginger. She sat up and took a sip. I smiled, knowing the chilled water had satisfied her. I waited for her *thank you* ....

"Leave."

"Uh ..." This was not the reaction I had pictured in my head at all. "But ..." I stalled, giving her a chance to rethink her command.

"Go away," she said as she set the glass of water on her bedside table and turned away, dismissing me.

Phooey.

Guess I don't need her appreciation. I should be used to this treatment by now, right?

CHAPTER 4

AN UNHAPPY BIRTHDAY

In my room … the safety of my room, now perfectly cleaned and the bed elegantly made, it showcased a serene setting for sleep and also served as a place to get things done. I decided to get serious about my plans for Filbert's rescue. I grabbed the construction paper and markers, glue sticks, and stickers from under my bed. I decided to use the bright-colored paper; they would really get noticed. As I put the supplies on my bed, I looked out of the corner of my eye and did a double take. Camellia, the arm strangler, was holding my hamster, Dookie, the same way she held my arm giving me that burn!

"Nooooo! Don't you touch my Dookie!" I ran over, grabbed Dookie out of her hands, and pushed her into my open closet.

I examined Dookie, closely surveying him for any damage. I held him to my ear and could feel and hear his itty-bitty heart racing as mine beat irregularly hard.

"It's okay, Dookie … it's okay," I murmured, holding him close to my chest.

Camellia was struggling to get up after my push. "I wasn't gonna hurt him," she said. Now she was standing in my bedroom, straightening her clothes.

She would not convince me. Now that I did remember her, I remembered her biting me too … many times. What kind of girl bites other girls? I never had the urge to bite anyone; this girl, however, seemed to be a baby vampire. Maybe she was a vampire. I quickly became suspicious when her full cheeks spread to a menacing grin. I imagined her shapeshifting into a fanged fiend feasting on poor, innocent youngsters.

"I'm not so sure of that," I told her. "You seem to like to hurt people and I will not let you touch my Dookie. Do you understand?" The boldness I acquired from my stay at The Children's Horrible House thankfully had come home with me.

"Touch your Dookie?" She giggled.

When she laughed she didn't seem as devilish. Actually, she had a cute laugh—which seemed strange coming from such a heinous monster.

"Is that really his name? Dookie?"

"Yup. You have a problem with that?" I really liked my newfound confidence.

"No, actually I think it's perfect. He kind of looks like a turd."

Ouch. I wasn't sure if I should be hurt or laugh with her.

"I think you should leave." I pointed, with Dookie in my hand, to my bedroom doorway.

After a second, she walked toward the door; instead of going out, she did a back flip attempt onto my bed, knocking some of the markers and papers off and onto the floor, yet still managing to get herself comfortable.

"Your room is so neat … I like the way you make your bed. It's so cozy."

I ruefully reached down to pick up the fallen supplies. I couldn't help feeling flattered by her compliments. I mean, my room and bed did look really good and made me proud to have someone else appreciate its current tidy state. My hand brushed the coverlet, ironing it flat as if I were a perfectionist.

"So, what have you been doing this summer?" she asked as she hiked a leg up and crossed it over her other knee. "My family and I went to my grandparents' lake house. We had a lot of fun. We ate lots of candy, had a campfire, went canoeing and fishing. I can't believe school is starting in two weeks. I'm excited. I have a lot of friends I haven't seen since school was out. There's so much to tell them. Where do you go to school?" She said all of this as if I should be interested in her life.

I answered her, hoping to end our conversation. "I'm going to a new school this year. It's small and private, called Compass Academy. You probably haven't heard of it."

She sat up like she had been jolted with electricity. "Of course I've heard of it, I'm going there too!" Her eyes grew into saucers of delight.

I wasn't sure why she'd be excited about my enrollment; evidently she had enough friends and if this was any indication about the quality of kids to be found in this new school, I was not excited.

"Holly! Could you come here?" my mom's voice called from downstairs.

I responded quicker than ever and ran to the kitchen. When I got there, all the lights were out except for the nine candles blazing on top of the cake. When I walked into the room, everyone including Ginger, Cashew, Hickory, my parents, and the Seedlings sang "Happy Birthday" to me. I blew out the candles—after I wished for a better birthday party next year.

CHAPTER 5

Meanwhile, at THE CHILDREN'S HORRIBLE HOUSE

Those two horrible kids were gone. However, the moment they left, Sirius Pankins regretted sending Holly and Coriander away. No other children had come so close to discovering the hidden treasure she knew was here. The twin boys and the girl, Clover, remained, but without Holly and Coriander, they proved useless in the quest.

The treasure had to be here. She could feel it. She banged her fist on her desk, jarring the librarian, who was supposedly her sister—make that half-sister.

"What was that for?" Willow, once known only as Miss Judge, asked.

"Oh, I was just thinking …"

"You think violently."

"I suppose so." Sirius relaxed back into her high-backed leather chair, reflecting about how she came so close, yet still had no definitive answers. And with her secret identity being exposed, she felt vulnerable in this new, fragile situation. She had to play nice with these people while continuing her search. Not long after their identities were uncovered, the two sisters had formed a truce in their relationship, both using one another for possible further gain, for now.

Sirius held the magnifying glass up to the book *Sage Themes*, searching for anything out of the ordinary to jump out at her and give her clues on the whereabouts of her hidden treasure. She flipped through *The Message*, the other big, heavy book found within the empty grave of her father's, and became bored. Why did the contents of these books look so ordinary? They were bold words that seemed to blend together, signifying nothing.

Sirius had always relied heavily on her intuition; so far it had never left her dissatisfied. Taciturnly, her sense wasn't telling her anything important at the moment. She tried to focus and gain some deeper understanding of the words she read over and over again. After her vision blurred, she stood and paced around in her office, giving up temporarily on studying useless blabbering books. Why did her father think this stuff was so interesting? Why did he record all this unnecessary information? Why couldn't it be easier? Couldn't he have condensed these notes? Even Miss Judge found these writings to be of little assistance.

"You know, the more I look at these books, I swear there is some kind of code, like everything written on these pages actually means something else."

"What do you think they mean?" Sirius asked Miss Judge.

"Hmm .... I'm not exactly sure. I wonder if they are even meant to be taken literally. You see, a lot of what is recorded is actual information, like a history or an instruction manual; it almost seems like this is to be understood metaphorically or symbolically in order to get the whole true meaning from the texts."

"So?"

"So, I'm not sure what it is really saying. If I am understanding it, it sounds almost ludicrous."

"Haven't you been studying this stuff your whole life?" Sirius asked, meaning it as a jab.

"I could ask you the same thing," Miss Judge quickly retorted. "Let me go back to the library to see if I can find any cross-referencing material to fill in these gaps." She stood up and left.

Sirius watched her leave and noticed Miss Judge (or Willow, her half-sister), had the same walk and build as her father, Hawthorne North Star. Miss Judge stood tall and long-legged, with a sturdy construction which held an ample amount of dignity. While Sirius too stood tall, she carried a lot of the svelte, graceful qualities of her mother, which she tried to repress. She was comfortable in her controlling position, although when alone, with no one to threaten, she became more open with herself.

Major Whoopins knocked before entering. Sirius positioned herself behind her desk and permitted Major Whoopins' entry.

"The kids is returned safe and sound at home, Miss Pankins," he proudly announced.

"Yes, thank you, but,"—she hesitated—"I'm thinking I may have been too hasty in their departure." She pensively tapped a pencil against her desktop.

"What you supposin'?" Major Whoopins asked.

"I'm not sure yet."

"Well, uh."

"That will be all. Thank you," she said, dismissing him.

CHAPTER 6

THE JALOPY

I had a restless night of sleep mixed with nightmarish images of my first day of school. I kept waking up worried all the kids would be mean bullies like Thistle and Nettle, the two jerks who loved tormenting me back at The Children's Horrible House. Why did kids have to be so mean? I never found any delight in making another kid feel bad. I preferred having fun and making kids laugh. I wondered if private school kids liked to laugh or if they were more hoity-toity. Why did my parents want to spend all this money we did not seem to have on my education? Oh, that's right. My dad had been offered a job teaching science there and my tuition was practically free.

I stayed in bed long after I awoke. I wanted to stay in bed all day … actually, forever. I knew that wasn't an option. I hesitantly decided to get up and get dressed in my weird new uniform—a collared white shirt and a blue skirt. Yes, a skirt … I hated skirts. My skinned-up knees protruded from the bottom and there was nothing glamorous about this poly-cotton pleated thing. I lifted the socks as high as they could go, hoping to cover my unsightly legs, and tried on my new brown loafers, as my mom called them. I looked in the mirror and stuck my tongue out at myself. I looked hideous—until I put on my bunny hat … yes, much better.

The only good thing about going to this new school was no more riding the bus. I thought for a second and concluded maybe that wasn't a good thing after all. My dad would be giving me a ride to school now, but not in my mom's newer Buick Riviera. Most likely, he would be driving me in one of his old, rusting, backfiring jalopies.

I was unfortunately right.

"Let's go, Holly!" my dad called out. He actually sounded excited.

I would have been less reluctant if I didn't see what car he pulled out to take me to school. Today he chose a once-red Impala that now resembled a dirt-colored rust bucket of bolts and wires.

He opened the door for me, which in itself was an accomplishment. To say it creaked open would be a great understatement. It growled and howled open and almost fell to the ground before my dad caught it and put it back on its hinges. I hopped in. The distinct smell of gasoline and old car filled my senses as he attempted to fire up the noisy engine. It took a couple of turns of the key, though, and when it caught, the engine roared to life.

We were about to leave when my mom came out and handed me my lunch box. "You almost forgot this," she said with a smile.

My eyes bulged and I had a delayed panic attack. What if I had gone to school with no lunch? My lunch was the only thing I really cared about, and if I had gone the whole day without it, I might have died.

"Thanks, Mom," I said with relief.

The seats in my dad's rust mobile were cushioned with fluff which was supposed to be covered by vinyl or fabric. The springs that poked through the stuffing could be fun to bounce on, although I had to be careful to not get stabbed. The dial on the radio was set all the way to the left. Distorted static, which was hard to hear over the loud rumbling engine, is what blared from the speakers. Judging by all the noise surrounding me, there would be very little chance I could pull up to my new school unobserved.

As we rambled into the driveway of Compass Academy, I noticed a lot of parents and students gathered near the front entry. The school was nowhere near as fancy as The Children's Horrible House; however, it wasn't ugly either. It was in an old church with a tall steeple and a cross that stood scratching the sky.

Parents seemed to be giving their children pep talks while some other kids were inching away from long index fingers pointing at their faces as their mom's fluffy heads rocked side to side. All their once undivided attention became securely focused on my father's big, ugly, loud car as it squeakily rolled past them and parked. The engine shut off, giving a powerful backfire that caused all the parents and students to drop to the ground in fear of what they must have thought was an explosion.

He looked over at me, gave me a big grin, and said, "Pretty good, huh?"

My dad thought the garishness was great. Some people want attention … most kids do, right? This was not the attention I wanted. I slid down on the seat, hoping everyone would go inside and not see me getting out.

"Let's go, Holly Hocks!" He opened the door for me again, not so much out of chivalry, more because the door could only be opened from the outside and the strength needed to push the button to make the door open wasn't what I or most normal people possessed. Good thing my dad was so strong.

Yes, everyone watched me get out of the car, and yes, everyone seemed to be snickering and snorting at my expense. I kept my eyes pointed to the ground as I walked toward the school—until I heard my name called out.

"Holly! Holly, it's me, Coriander."

Coriander? Could it really be him? Then from behind a nice, tall, brown-haired mom came Coriander.

He stood there, shyly mismatched by a sure yet crooked grin on his face. I bounced up to him and thought about giving him a big hug. I wasn't sure if he might be grossed out, so I stood there awkwardly, too.

My father, being the ever opposite of shy, introduced himself to Coriander and his mother.

Extending his hand for shaking, my dad said, "Hello, ma'am … young man. I am Mr. Spinatsch, and whom might you be?"

Coriander shook his hand while his mother did the talking.

"Hello Mr. Spinatsch. This is Coriander, and I am his mother, Mrs. Oats."

They kept talking as Coriander and I sheepishly looked at each other, not sure if we should talk with parents around to hear about our recent adventure. Did they know about The Children's Horrible House or not? I mean, they did threaten to send me there. Though when I came back home, they acted like I had never left. They never even asked me about my visit. Time must have been suspended while

I was away and picked right back up as soon as I woke up on top of my bed. I wanted to ask Coriander about time suspension, dimensions, or warps, but it would have to wait until we could be alone.

"Don't just stand there looking weird, Coriander. Aren't you going to talk to your friend?" His mother gently prodded him on the butt.

It must have embarrassed him, because he turned away and walked into the school without looking back.

"Cute hat," his mom said, and smiled at me. She must have felt embarrassed too, and tried to ease her discomfort with a compliment.

"Thank you," I said as I peeked up at my dad, who was checking the time on his watch.

"Nice to meet you, Mrs. Oats. I better not be late for my first day of school. Maybe I'll see your son in my class," my dad said with a polite smile.

I wondered how it would be if Coriander was a student of my dad's.

CHAPTER 7

FOURTH GRADE

School is school, no matter where you go, I found, except at The Children's Horrible House. There we learned about exciting subjects like astronomy, meteorology, and horticulture. I thought back to the amazing night when Jupiter and Venus aligned with Regulus, to form the bright Star of Panivita. Seeing such a spectacular show right before my eyes was something I could never forget.

Here at Compass Academy, schoolwork was back to the repetitious grind of vocabulary words, multiplication tables, science, and history. History was one of those subjects that was somewhat interesting yet still had the overwhelming power to put me to sleep.

BAM!

I woke with a start. I saw a pile of books on the floor next to my desk and the feet of Miss Tinkles right in front of the books. My gaze traveled up and I saw her empty hands which once held the stack of books still poised after the completion of their mission.

"Awake?" she asked.

"Uh-huh, yes, ma'am." I stretched my eyelids open.

"Stay that way," she said as she turned around and sashayed back to the front of the classroom.

Immediately my eyes closed and struggled to reopen. Staying awake was not going to be easy.

I could feel other eyes staring at me and saw the disturbing gaze of Camellia. She looked around the classroom and then back to me with a strange grin. She held out her hands and gave my arm a telepathic Indian burn, all while keeping a steady glare in my direction.

She was so weird.

CHAPTER 8

U.F.L

Lunch should be easy, right? I had the hang of how things worked in most schools; however, the first day of school, lunchtime always presented its own form of obstacles, mainly in the seating department. If you sat with the wrong people, you could become pegged forever. I never based my friendships on popularity, so that wasn't the problem. I was more conscious of getting leeched onto by someone who might be hard to get away from after you've had the life sucked out of you. My parents always stressed to pick good friends. They joked, saying, *You can pick your friends and you can pick your nose, but you can't pick your friend's nose.* I had zero desire to pick anyone's nose, so that warning was fun yet totally unnecessary.

I was excited about my lunch today, so it made little difference with whom I sat. I looked for Coriander; he hadn't been in any of my classes and I still didn't see him in the lunchroom. Camellia waved to me, trying to get my attention; I pretended not to see her.

My mom let me pack my own lunch, which is why I was so happy about it. I was sick of her pot-luck lunches. She had a tendency to get awfully creative when it came to edible combinations; nothing went together, in my opinion. One time she packed me a lunch of liverwurst on rye and an apple with more bruises than a boxer.

The worst was when she packed me a UFL (unidentified fried leftovers). Yuck!

Oh, I almost forgot .... Another time, she gave me a cream cheese and jelly on pumpernickel.

Pumpernickel .... Pumpernickel is the grossest bread ever, and I couldn't risk being disgusted anymore so I took matters into my own hands. I made a beautiful shaved-turkey and American cheese sandwich on soft grain bread. For sides, I packed applesauce, yogurt-covered raisins, a snack cake, and chocolate milk. I set them out on the folded napkin I had given myself, when a girl with the coolest sneakers I had ever seen walked by looking for a place to sit. Her sneakers were pink and raspberry with Velcro straps—I wanted them. They stood out among the sea of brown loafers most all the other kids wore. They looked supercool and like they could go really fast. She moseyed deeper into the pool of full tables and then, as if she could sense the emptiness of mine, she turned around. She seemed unsure if she should come over. I smiled and patted the empty space next to me, inviting her to dine. She accepted and set down her lunch box and backpack.

"I'm Holly. What's your name?"

Her lips twitched and then she said, "Conifer."

"Hi, Conifer," I said, watching her start to unpack her lunch.

She had a thermos filled with some sort of soup, half a bagel, red licorice sticks, and a juice bottle. The juice bottle looked good and sugary, something my mom never bought. When I looked back at my assortment, my lunch was obviously yummier.

"How's your soup?" I asked after I finished my sandwich.

"It's okay .... There's all these little rabbis in there."

"Rabbis? What are rabbis?" I asked.

She showed me the inside of her thermos. It was dark, but I could see a brownish broth and some little noodles.

I looked at her and asked, *"Rabbis?"*

We both laughed. The word sounded funny to us, even though we had no idea what *rabbi* actually meant.

"Hey, where did you get your sneakers and how come you are allowed to wear them?" I asked.

"Um,"—her eyes searched her memory bank—"I can't remember where I found them, but I do know I have to go and get the right brown loafers today. Apparently, we can wear jeans and sneakers on Fridays only and in gym class."

"Oh." I couldn't wait to go shopping to find those sneakers.

She licked her lips and then used the backside of her wrist to wipe off her mouth. She asked, "Who's your favorite teacher so far?"

"Favorite teacher?" I hadn't even thought about it. None of these teachers were as exciting as the teachers back at The Children's Horrible House. I thought about Miss Spelling and how she enlightened us on so many things, especially about gardening and how to plant by the moon's lunar cycles. The teachers here taught ordinarily—like their appearances. Not like Miss Spelling and her half-moon-shaped eyes, or Miss Guide who could have passed for a comet streaming across the night sky, or even Miss Judge, the librarian whose hair flowed like lava.

I thought about Miss Tinkles. The only remarkable feature about her face was her teeth. Instead of being bucked out, they slanted in.

Like I said, nothing remarkable here.

"I don't have one yet. Haven't met all of them."

"My favorite is Mr. Snorton, the music teacher. He's really funny. Did you have music yet?"

"Not yet, but now I'm excited to meet Mr. Snorton." I giggled and Conifer joined in, spitting out some of her noodles, which of course caused us to laugh harder.

CHAPTER 9

THANKS ENGLISH …

Miss Tinkles decided it would be a good idea to get the class engaged by asking us to stand up and spell words that made up our spelling list. Most first days of school planned more introductory exercises; however, at this new school they went straight to the lessons. Miss Tinkles called out a word and if you thought you could spell it, you were to raise your hand and then stand and spell it out loud. I was reluctant to stand up and speak out loud, much less spell a word out loud, so I let the more confident kids go first.

"Catastrophe," Miss Tinkles called out.

What was she thinking? What kind of word was *catastrophe* and how in the world did you spell it?

A girl wearing her prim-collared shirt covered in a smart-looking sweater raised her hand and was called on. I noticed her brown, otherwise boring, hair curled under, including her heavy bangs that made her look sophisticated for her age.

She spelled out, "C-A-T-A-S-T-R-O-P-H-E."

WRONGGGG … I snidely said to myself. It couldn't end in an *e*.

Most likely, it ended in *y.* I couldn't wait for the teacher to give her the correct spelling. This poor girl would probably feel really stupid. A hint of concern came over me as I imagined the hurt she would feel at being so obviously wrong.

"Correct. Thank you, Melia," Miss Tinkles said.

HUH? That was correct? I promptly became nervous. What kind of school was this, a place for geniuses? I was no genius, I knew this for a fact.

"Indentured," Miss Tinkles called out.

These words weren't getting any easier. How was I going to participate if I hadn't even heard of these words?

One boy who had a really bad haircut was called on.

He cleared his throat and recited the letters. "I-N-D-E-N-C-H-O-R-E-D," he said.

Sounds correct to me ....

"Incorrect. Anyone else want to give it a try?" Miss Tinkles asked.

HUH? I was stunned. *Not me,* I thought. My gaze followed Miss Tinkles' eyes, searching for the next speller. She came close to looking into mine, when a girl wearing a headgear contraption raised her hand. After Miss Tinkles called on her, she stood and pulled hard on her underwear, releasing it from her butt cheeks. The tug and release was an interesting sight considering most of the class had now witnessed this girl digging into her butt. This was the kind of girl I liked—an unashamed butt-picker.

"Umm … I-N-D … ind" (she whispered to herself) "C-H-U-R-D." The girl looked hopefully at Miss Tinkles.

"No?" Miss Tinkles said although it sounded more like a question.

After the butt-picker misspelled the word also, Miss Tinkles spelled it for us. She called out another word and this one was easy. *Oooo*, I knew I could spell this one. I raised my hand and flapped it around in the air, confident in my ability. I would not look stupid today.

Miss Tinkles called on me and I stood up. I spelled the word inside my head and checked the arrangement. It all checked out. After I cleared my throat as I had seen so many other mature people do before they spoke, I was ready.

"S-O-R-D, sword." I even said the word after to let her know I was finished.

"Incorrect," she stated.

Huh? How is that possibly wrong? I was utterly confounded.

"Anyone else want to give it a try?" she said while looking around the room.

I looked too, and dared anyone else to spell this word. *Sword* was a word I was highly familiar with, and to know I somehow misspelled it made me rethink my whole prior educational upbringing.

"I will, Miss Tinkles," Melia said.

"Go ahead."

"S-*W*-O-R-D," Melia said, and stared at me when she accentuated the *W*. Okay, maybe she didn't stare and it was more of a glance, but she didn't have to gloat. *Geez.*

I said it in my head. *Sword*? Where did that *w* come from? All the phonics rules that had been drilled into my head years before were now being outlawed. Guess I was stupid … like all these other kids …. except for Melia.

CHAPTER 10

YOU'RE A GRAND OLD FLAG

I was glad when the spelling *catastrophe* was over and we headed into music class. The door swung open to expose a sun-bleached room with rays flashing from the large window, into a space with bleachers like a gymnasium on a much smaller scale. The teacher was a well-dressed, bearded man who seemed eager to hear us sing. Mr. Snorton arranged us in order, tallest in the back and shortest in the front. Of course I was in the back with the boys. Coriander came in a little late, and Mr. Snorton put him in the back row next to me. I was immediately happy and decided Mr. Snorton was my favorite teacher, too. Coriander and I were afraid to talk to each other, yet we both exchanged a side-eye of excitement.

Mr. Snorton pushed Play on the tape recorder, and from the rectangular speakers blared a song called, "You're a Grand Old Flag." Mr. Snorton sang along while flinging his fingers around with the beat.

When the song was over, he asked, with a smile, "What do you think? Fun, right?"

The class collectively shrugged, some reluctantly agreed, while a couple of others sarcastically said, "It was just simply grand!"

"This happens to be one of my personal favorites. This song has been around since 1906. It was first a play production, and this song quickly caught on and sold over one million copies in sheet music. We are going to learn a simple march and some other songs, and perform them for your parents at our first open house."

Mr. Snorton had told us this as if we should be excited too. Some of the kids in the front rows actually did seem excited. Coriander and I didn't love the idea.

* * *

The best part of school is when it's over and I was so thankful when the final bell rang. The only thing that stood between me and some good old afternoon television fun was this loud, stinky ride home in my dad's automobile-ish-like thing and my homework. Yes, homework … even on the first day. I think *that* should be outlawed.

In order for my brain to properly function, I needed some snacks in my gut. I asked my mom what we had to eat. *Boy, was that a bad idea.*

She opened the refrigerator, rustled the items around, and listed the contenders. "Well, we have mayonnaise, onions, peanut butter, here's some spinach … oh, and tomatoes, celery sticks, and some mushrooms. And we have some leftover broccoli, lasagna and applesauce."

My mom always rambled off a list of foods that did not go

together and collectively, they all sounded disgusting.

"Never mind, I'll find something," I said as I searched through the cupboards.

I found some potato chips and started snacking on those right away, yet knew I needed more. I grabbed the peanut butter and sliced an apple and put a dab on each slice. As I was eating, Hickory sprang in, singing in his usual incomprehensible fashion. He scooped a couple of my chips and threw them into his mouth, chewed a little, smiled, and carried on.

Even though he burped, farted, and sang tuneless melodies, Hickory was actually exceptionally smart. He had all "A"s throughout his school years. Plus, he never needed a calculator; he could do multiplication and long division in his head. In fact, he was so smart he didn't need to go to college. At least that's what he said after he spent two months at the local community college. He decided he would own his own business, and going to college only taught him how to work for someone else. He decided, instead of wasting all that time and money on school, he could get a head start on becoming a millionaire by starting a lawn care service called Hickory's Harvest Lawn Care … the slogan was "You grow; we mow."

"How was your day, honey?" my mom asked, stepping back into the kitchen.

I shrugged.

"Have any homework?"

She knew I had homework. I could tell, but to test her I shook my head.

"No homework? I don't believe it."

How do moms know? I must have given off some sort of guilty look.

"C'mon, let's go. Get it done. No nothing until your homework is finished."

"No nothing?"

"Nope. Nothing."

"Mom, I need new sneakers." I threw that in, hoping to derail her from the "no nothing" train of thought.

"Already? Your feet do grow quickly. … We don't have much money right now, though."

"Can't you just write a check?" I asked, clearly not understanding the way money worked.

She laughed a little and gave me a little pat on my head, saying, "Not exactly. And if you don't do your homework, you'll get nothing."

Derailment was not meant to be. I went to work and after I looked up the definitions of the vocabulary words in the dictionary and made a set of multiplication flash cards, I looked around for Juniper. I hadn't seen her in a while. I found Ginger in her bed, reading a book, as usual. Next to her, in abundant luxury, was her kitty cat, Sugar Snap, and her new batch of kittens. Sugar Snap had been pregnant at least a hundred twenty thousand times and she always had the exact, same-looking kittens. Half the batch matched an Orange Creamsickle and the other half of the kittens looked like an Oreo Cookie ice cream flurry, even though Sugar Snap was a white Siamese. Sugar Snap was giving her new kittens a thorough bath, and I wanted to go in and give each of them a cuddle but wasn't sure how to gain access with Ginger there.

"Have you seen Juniper?" I asked her.

"Have you found Filbert?" she retorted.

Filbert! I almost forgot about that dumb dog. I was going to make some "missing posters" and put an ad in the paper; I must have been distracted somehow. In an instant I felt a weight of guilt wrap its heaviness around me.

"I need to make some posters and put an ad in the lost-and-found." I started to go make up for my failures.

"Don't bother. Basil already did all that," she said as flatly as voices can speak.

"Oh."

Now I couldn't even make up for my laziness. I felt like I disappointed Ginger; even more, I failed Clover. Now what was I going to do? Would I ever see her or the twins again?

I *did* see Coriander today, which gave me hope—although we never had a chance to speak. Tomorrow would be different … hopefully.

CHAPTER 11

Back at THE CHILDREN'S HORRIBLE HOUSE

As Sirius skulked past the large, ornate oval mirror hanging on the wall, from the corner of her eye something or someone else stared out from the reflection and it spooked her. She was almost too afraid to look.

Slowly she stepped in front of it. At first everything seemed normal. She looked at herself and then suddenly her mother, Sings-in-the-Meadow, was looking back at her and it jolted Sirius from her ease. The strange reflection wasn't the only thing that puzzled her. Sirius had always known she resembled her mother, but ....

Then she saw the reflection in the background. The mirrored image wasn't her desk and chair, her lamp, or the other wall. Behind her mother was a cave filled with luminescent crystals jutting in all directions. Her mother stood still in the midst of the beautiful geometrical spires as Sirius' body moved, searching for what might be behind her. Sirius closed her eyes only for an instant. When she opened them, the image in the mirror was only her own.

Did she imagine the whole scene? Was she going crazy? The air felt stale, and Sirius felt as if the solid walls in her office had caused a sudden bout of claustrophobia. Her breath became quick and she felt faint.

She immediately left, and felt better in the fresh air while she wandered through her home. She peeked into the rooms which used to serve much different purposes and in small instances had flashbacks to those scenes from her past.

She liked that *her* wing of the home was still mostly untouched, not reconstructed to fit the needs of so many children. What if all the children left and returned home? Would she miss them? Having them here was some kind of weird comfort. Her self-made Sirius Pankins identity was built on being the intimidating force in charge of this place. She enjoyed the power that came with it; still, she felt something was missing. She found herself going around the house with no particular destination, when her body stopped in front of the door leading to the attic.

Sirius opened the door and climbed the steep, creaking stairs. When she stepped to the top, she had an instant flashback to her childhood. The bright yellow painted walls and slanted roof sections opened to an enchanted playroom which had stayed remarkably like the way she had seen it last. This place had been her sanctuary for many years, and now it seemed like running into an old, dear friend. She envisioned a silhouetted version of herself as a little girl prancing around the giant space … going from one area to another like a hummingbird. The scent of dried flowers dusted in powder fueled her nostalgia and she became entranced by its power. She breathed it in, hoping for it to take her back in time when her mother was still here. She held out her hands, hoping to conjure her mother's spirit—accidentally knocking over an antique broom, which jolted her out of her enchantment. It crashed to the floor in a show of unnecessary dramatic clamor. For a moment, Sirius felt embarrassed by her dalliance in the past, as well as her clumsiness. She picked up the old broom and set it against the wall, making sure of its stance.

She glanced around and found the dollhouse sitting in its spot, waiting—hurt by her not noticing it first. It really was a magnificent structure. She bent over and peered in all the little rooms. It seemed much smaller than she remembered, yet still it was quite grand. She had never seen a toy that matched the quality, craftsmanship, and grandeur this dollhouse presented. It was beautiful.

She remembered the day her father gave it to her. He had her blindfolded as he guided her up the attic stairs, and when they reached the top he removed the blinding cloth. When her eyes adjusted, her mother, Sings-in-the-Meadow, was standing behind a large structure and she pulled off a sheet that covered this amazing dollhouse. It had been the best gift ever. Sirius had quickly scuttled over to it and peered inside with a smile beaming from her face. Her mother stood at the opposite window and waved through the glass. Sirius now waved at the imaginary image of her mother. In this moment, her identity flickered as if her former childhood persona, Saffron, was reaching out from the death Sirius had inflicted upon herself.

Sirius shook her head, gaining her composure, and beheld the male doll all alone in the study. She remembered placing him there as a child, right before she stopped playing in the attic. *Had no one played with this house since then?* she wondered. How come she hadn't been up here in so long? She had been too focused on her devious plans to come visit her memories. The study was the last place she saw her father, and he was represented by this doll in the same spot.

She picked up the doll and sat back on the floor. She stared into the doll's face as her father's image came to mind. He had kind eyes, always, and even though she knew she had disappointed him so many times, he always met her gaze with approval. How could she have been so selfish? Why couldn't she see how badly she hurt him by being bad to herself and unkind to his staff? Something was happening within Sirius' coldhearted demeanor and it made her uncomfortable.

Sirius stood, about to depart from this trip through memory lane when, instead, she stepped down the small set of stairs leading to her tiny playroom. As a child, she had called it her Rainbow Room. A lot of times the sun came through a crystal which hung right in front of the window, sending rainbows dancing throughout the room. She searched for it dangling at the end of the cord, but the crystal was gone. She had never given a thought to that crystal before; but because it was missing, she was bothered.

She walked to the old, wavy-glassed window and saw the string that used to hold the crystal ... cut. She lifted the frayed cord and inspected the newness of its disseverment. Someone had cut it. Who would do that? And why?

Going through the list of people who had access to this room, Sirius realized it could have been anybody. Everyone was suspect and her first person of interest was in the library. Someone was a little too sneaky for the likes of Sirius Pankins. She decided to keep a closer eye on that librarian. Then something else caught her attention—the Star family tree. In a wooden framed picture, on various branches, family names stemmed from her father's lineage. To most people these names meant little and, even to her, most of them appeared inconsequential, for she had little knowledge of them. Sirius had not glanced at this picture in years. Her focus immediately went to the blank spot above her own name: Saffron Radiant Star. Her mother's name was noticeably absent from the tree. She pondered this inconsistency as she stared at another name … Willow Faint Star.

CHAPTER 12

IMPORTANT BOOKS

Sirius descended the stairs and quietly shut the door behind her. As she approached the library, she could hear some muttering voices behind the walls. She tried to listen carefully; still, she couldn't make out any clear identities. After she opened the double doors, everything went silent, as if the mutterings detected her and stopped. Where was Willow, or Miss Judge, as she was formally regarded? She looked around for her and strangely found no one. Sirius wandered through the aisles and became overwhelmed by the sheer amount of books held in this space.

Why did some people think books were so important? Sirius couldn't understand. If you had something to say, why not simply say it? Did everything have to be written and recorded? Why were there so many varied writers? Couldn't they think of something more interesting to do? How special did these authors think they were? As if everyone wants to read what they thought about. *Who cares?* Sirius thought. There was something beautiful in the temporal—the fleeting thought or the conversation between two people not to be shared with anyone, not to be recorded for everyone to read and feel diminished by the shared unoriginal thoughts. Are there any unique thoughts, special to one being? Or are there only universal thoughts floating around in a dimension where consciousness dwells, traveling around from one person's head to another, sharing commonality? Sirius lived in the moment and had no time to read the boring messages writers felt compelled to leave, as a message in a bottle to all those unlucky people who are curious enough to peek inside the pages of their souls.

Her contemplative brooding brought her in front of the one gigantic arched window that took up the whole west-facing wall. She felt drawn to this vantage point every time she was in this room. Gazing at her oak tree she saw, to the right, her garden. The sun was setting and the orange light fought to stay above the horizon in beams that reached across the sky. The light played with the linear clouds, making them appear in delirious shades of broken coral, dark dripping raspberry, and melting cotton-candy pink. Since she found little action in this room, she wandered back to her bedroom, still restless. She went back to her office to see if she missed anything, but still found nothing to entice her. Would she ever feel appeased?

CHAPTER 13
UNEATEN CRUMBS

"Wonda' where they took Corianda and Holly?" Clover asked in her thick New England accent.

"Yeah, I thought we would find them by now," Staniel stated in his scratchy voice.

Danley said, "I checked everywhere: the glowing garden, THE DUNGEON, the hanging cage—and their bunks are empty."

"Cleaned out," Staniel said, swiping his hands against each other.

"You think we could ask Maja Whoopins?" Clover wondered aloud.

"Not sure he'll tell us," Danley said, shaking his head.

Clover said, "Can't hurt to ask."

"Oh, yes it could ..." Staniel pointed to Director Pankins, who was passing the dining hall, and then he pointed to his own butt.

The three of them shared a collective shiver and tried to finish their lunches.

"It's been lonely here without them," Clover said. She set down her food, having trouble finishing the meal.

"You gunna eat that?" Staniel put his hands around her hoagie, ready to devour her uneaten sandwich.

"Nah, you can have it."

"Hey!" Danley protested.

Staniel regarded Danley, and broke off half and gave it to his twin brother. Danley silently thanked him and ate it.

Clover peeked back at Miss Shapen, who was making sure no crumbs went uneaten, and decided the twins could finish the rest of her lunch … though she had to be careful, or she might not get any food the next day if she appeared ungrateful. She pretended to eat her fruit medley as she passed the dish over to the twins, who gobbled it like baby birds.

"Where's your ugly friend?" Clover heard coming from behind her. She turned to see Thistle and Nettle elbowing each other, proud of their insult.

"You guys must ask each otha' that same question all the time," Clover said, with a smirk attached.

Staniel and Danley giggled, their fat cheeks filled with Clover's food.

Thistle and Nettle weren't used to her wit, and snarled their noses, looking even uglier as they sauntered away.

"You know who else I haven't seen in a while?" Clover asked.

"Who?" the twins asked.

"Cherry."

"Do you miss her?" Staniel asked.

"A little, and with Holly gone and Thistle and Nettle always lookin' to be annoyin', I miss havin' an ally."

"We're still here," Danley said.

"And *we* are your allies," Staniel affirmed.

Clover couldn't help but smile. "Thanks, guys," she said. Her stomach grumbled with annoyance at her blatant treachery of not feeding it. "Oh, *now* you're hungry," she said while rolling her eyes at her stomach.

Danley asked, "Who are you talking to?"

"My stomach."

"Do that often?" Staniel asked. "Do you talk to your butt too?"

"No, but I've heard you talk out of your butt," Clover said.

With her triumphant comeback, Danley tried to contain his laughter.

"I've heard *your* butt talk, too," Clover said to Danley, and made fart noises with her mouth as all three of them fell into hysterics.

CHAPTER 14
COTTON BALLS

Tuesdays and Thursdays, in addition to the recess on odd days, we had physical education. Coriander was in this class with me. I was so excited when I saw him, and he acted happy too.

"Hey, Holly," he said.

"Hey, Coriander," I said.

"I can't believe you go here too."

"Have you been going to this school for a while?" I asked.

"No, this is my first year. We moved here over the summer."

"Where did you used to live?"

"About two hours north of here, in a small town called Viburnum Valley."

"Sounds pretty."

"Yeah, I guess."

I asked, "Hey, have you heard from Clover or Staniel and Danley?"

"I was about to ask you the same thing."

"Gosh, I wonder where they live? I wonder if they live far away?"

"Who knows?" Coriander shrugged.

"So, what have you been doing?"

Coriander leaned in close to me. "Planning to get back to you know where … ASAP," he said in a whisper through cupped hands so no one could read his lips.

"Really? You're going to go back? Why?"

"Are you serious? You don't want to go back?"

"I'm a little scared. That place was a tad frightening. Especially, you know who. … Yet, now that I think about it, it would be kind of cool to go back … even if only to see everyone."

Coriander seemed to have something else on his mind. "I know the treasure is there, still. I bet Director Pankins doesn't know where it is either. Even Miss Judge doesn't know how to find it. But I think I do. I've been going over all the things we learned about and, yes, there are still some missing pieces of important information. I think we could figure it all out somehow, if I could just get back."

Coach Cotton blew his whistle. We all lined up and did some warm-up exercises: jumping jacks, squats, and sit-ups. We ran some laps around the field too. Coach Cotton was obviously really into soccer. He always carried at least one soccer ball under an arm. The black-and-white ball placed by his side was held there effortlessly, which is how he gained the nickname Coach Cotton Balls. He had us in one long line and, based on our stature, placed us in the appropriate positions. After each person was assigned their post, he whistled, indicating the finality of his decisions.

"Iris, you're midfielder … ***FLURRRP.***" (That's the sound the whistle made.)

"Loriope, you're right halfback … ***FLURRRP.***"

"Oleander, right cornerback … ***FLURRRP.***" And so on ….

Somehow I became the goalie. I guarded the net with all I had.

However, that didn't keep those balls from flying past me. Coriander was good at soccer. He could move the ball around his feet like magic. The ball seemed to stay with him like some kind of magnetic force as he bounced the ball around the field with his feet, knees, and head, faster than my eyes could keep up. I was glad he was on my team.

CHAPTER 15
THE LURKING PRESENCE

I grew into the school routine naturally and since I had a new habit of making my bed every morning, going to bed felt special every night. I looked forward to pulling down my clean sheets and climbing into bed. I could see into Dookie's cage from my bed and watch him nudging around in his chips. Last Christmas, Juniper had given me a night-light which sent sparkles around my room and it resembled fairy dust floating through the air.

I missed Juniper. Where was she? I hadn't seen her in a while. I knew she had a new boyfriend, but *geez*. She had to come home sometime soon.

As I drifted off to sleep, my consciousness went on its own journey. All at once, I was floating around my house in a space suit. There was no gravity keeping me on the ground, yet I never flew higher than a couple of feet. I knocked into walls without any pain or sound. I was in a vacuum with suspended gravity, and still in my house. Everything was in its place, as usual … then gravity was restored and I was now walking around the house, looking for everyone. I was alone in my big, old, squeaky house. The house grew much bigger and scarier than normal. It felt empty, yet conversely inhabited by something other than me and my family. I could feel a presence. The only light I could see came from my room—at the distant end of the hallway, which eerily stretched to hundreds of feet long. I slowly slogged up the stairs and stood, scared to walk past each doorway, nevertheless still proceeding. Along the way, I felt something lurking behind each door. I reached the doorway to my room, and saw my night-light shining so brightly. I thought I should feel some relief, but I was still troubled by something.

On my hands and knees, I slowly crawled, trying to be extra quiet, back into bed. When I almost relaxed, I realized the loitering something was right outside my door! I could feel it circling and jerking back and forth. It was a shark! And it was thrashing its killer body to and fro, ready to come and tear me into shreds with its razor-sharp teeth. I closed my eyes, hoping I wouldn't see it attack me. When nothing happened, I opened them and saw the shark floating out in the hallway the exact same way I had been floating earlier. I was terrified of its long nose and sharp teeth. While zigging and zagging in circles, the shark readied to dart and eat me …

I woke from my nightmare and saw the gentle sparkles dancing around my room. I was still spooked, even too afraid to sit up. I knew that shark was still outside my door … waiting. And if he saw me sit up, he would come and get me. My breath quickened, and sweat was tickling my back as it ran down my sides. I reached within my soul and grabbed ahold of some courage and croaked out my mother's name. After I said it, I knew she wouldn't have been able to hear it.

"Mom," I called out louder.

"Mo-om," I called again, giving it even more boldness.

"Yes, honey?" My mother's tired voice came from her bedroom.

"I had a bad dream." My lower lip protruded and I wanted to cry.

"It's okay, honey. Go back to sleep."

"But …."

"Go to sleep," my dad ordered.

Any more calling for my mom was useless. I was on my own. I scanned the hallway, searching for the shadow of the shark. All I could see was the faint glow coming from my sparkling night-light. Slowly I realized that a shark or anything else swimming in my hallway was highly unlikely and I could rest assured of my safety from being gobbled up by a house shark. As time moved me further away from my nightmare, fear had less of a grip on me. I thought about more pleasant things … like goldfish and sea turtles … and I drifted off on the waves of sweet slumber.

CHAPTER 16
JUST A TRIM

Cashew's Halloween play was tonight, and I was extra excited. I loved having a reason to go out on the town. Soon we all would pile in one of my dad's less horrible cars and take in a great show. I could barely stand to eat my dinner. I wanted to hurry and get ready. I shoved the buttered spinach and spaghetti down my throat and excused myself.

I dressed in my favorite *Oscar the Grouch* T-shirt and corduroys and took a look in the mirror. I still had some sauce on my face that I cleaned off with a washrag. I checked my teeth to make sure no spinach was lingering between them, like Director Pankins had the first day I met her. I observed my hair color was not as bright as it used to be and it was a little long in the front. I blew out of my mouth, lifting my bangs, and decided I should give myself a little trim so I would look fantastic for Cashew's play. I dug around in the drawers and found some scissors and carefully cut my bangs. After I finished, I stepped back and saw my bangs looked crooked, so I cut off a little more. Still crooked … so I cut off *A LOT* more, until I had no more bangs ….

Phooey.

I didn't exactly look fantastic … I actually looked ridiculous. I decided to show off my new haircut anyway. I proudly went downstairs, showcasing my new do, when my mom practically spit her food across the table and followed that with an emotional yelp. Actually, her expression sounded more like "***AUWWPHHH!*** Oh, Holly! What have you done?"

"I wanted to look nice for Cashew's play tonight," I said.

"Not possible for a pustulating goiter like you," Ginger said. "Even if you didn't just butcher your bangs."

"And you're not wearing that," my mom said as she pointed to my outfit.

"What do you mean?" I asked, wondering what could be wrong with this perfectly great outfit.

"*What do you mean?*" Ginger mimicked. "*I'm Holly, and I like to wear boy's dirty clothes every day.*"

"They're not dirty," I protested.

"You're not wearing that," my mom said affirmatively.

"Then, what?" I asked, knowing I had nothing else except my ugly uniform.

"You can wear that pretty dress Aunt Lily sent you."

"That? Dress? No! I don't want to wear that ugly dress," I said.

"It is not ugly. It is very pretty, and you *will* wear it, understand?"

My mom was rarely firm, but I could see there was no use in arguing, especially with everybody else on her side.

I stomped back upstairs and sat on my bed, waiting till the last possible minute before changing. I scrutinized my open closet. The light at the top shined like a spotlight on the dress that hung there taunting me as if it knew I never, ever wanted to wear it. Mostly black, with small pink and yellow flowers, the hideous thing even had some lace trim in the front and, if you asked me, the whole ensemble was ugly. Aunt Lily, one of my favorite aunts, had so sweetly given it to me, along with a five-dollar bill. I was happy about the cash; however, I never intended to wear the dress.

My mom came in, ready to make me comply with her command. With an evident frown, I silently let her dress me.

As I rambled down the stairs, everyone waited at the bottom, making a big deal about how great I appeared.

"Don't you look so sweet, Holly." My dad smiled.

"I am not sweet," I muttered.

"So, you are a girl, after all," Hickory said, and belched.

"I'm not so sure about that; a dress doesn't make a girl," Ginger snapped as she waved her skirt around to indicate the *real* girl in the room was her. "Doesn't she have any better shoes to wear other than those sneakers?"

Everyone looked at my sneakers and then looked at my dress and decided to stay quiet about the clashing ensemble.

"You look great," my mother chirped.

I knew what I looked like and it was not great. I pulled my bunny ears down, trying to hide my face as we drove to the show.

When we walked inside the lobby of the theater, a photographer had set up a booth for families to have their portraits taken. Of course my family wanted their picture taken, so everyone took their position, ready to pose for the picture. The photographer was twisting the lens, trying to focus, when he peeked around his camera and stared at me.

"Might want to lose the hat," he said, as if his suggestion was an option.

I was NOT going to pose for this picture in this ugly dress and fresh bang-butchery without the protection of my bunny hat.

Ginger ripped my hat from my head, and the jerk photographer started snapping away. Turned out, most of the pictures were of me trying to get my hat back. The one my parents framed was of me with a firm upside-down sad face and everyone else smiling like denture models.

* * *

One day I couldn't take looking at that picture anymore. I had glanced at it too many times and hated it. I looked ridiculous. I wanted to hide it, and headed to the attic with it.

Cashew snuck up, causing me to jump. "What are you doing, Holly?"

"Oh, nothing," I said.

"Nothing? It looks like you're hiding that picture. Why?"

" 'Cause I'm ugly and I hate it," I truthfully told him.

"Holly, come here," he replied. "I need to tell you something very important."

I followed him to my room. We both sat on my bed and he looked straight at me. "Holly, I know I've told you this before, but maybe I wasn't clear. I know you feel like you're ugly now, but I want you to know something, and what I'm about to tell you is very, very important, *but* you'll have to be patient to see it come true." He paused. "One day, maybe a couple of years from now, you will blossom into a beautiful flower. Right now you are a seed being fed by Mom and Dad and all of us in our family garden. But one day, when the time is right, and with the right nurturing, you will bloom into a beautiful girl … I promise you."

I had heard him say this before, but it still shocked me to think that one day I might not be ugly and might actually be beautiful—if what my brother, Cashew, said was true.

"Do you believe me?" he asked.

Cashew never lied.

"Yes," I said. "Thank you, Cashew."

CHAPTER 17

SILLY BILLY'S

Conifer and I spent most weekends at one another's house, much to our mothers' dismay. When I was at her house, I took notice of Conifer's neat bedroom. Her bed was always made and her house was kept tidy. She must have already gone to The Children's Horrible House, or maybe her family was naturally neat.

Conifer's extraordinarily old grandfather lived with them too, in what was once their garage. We barely saw him, although once in a while I could hear him shuffling around the kitchen with the aid of his walker. It had green tennis balls at the bottom of each foot, to help it scoot along the floor. Conifer called him Poppy, but he couldn't hear a thing.

For some reason, Conifer and I became wrestle maniacs when we were together. We rolled around on any floor, giggling from one end of the house to the other, putting each other in various holds until one or the other gave up. Even though Conifer was skinny as a stick, she wrestled like a pro, which made it more fun for us; though not so much for her mother, who yelled at us in the middle of our mayhem.

At night we were supposed to go to sleep; instead, Conifer put on a scary movie. First of all, I do not like scary movies. I like goofy comedies, adventures, and light mysteries, not scary movies. But this wasn't my house and I didn't make the rules. Anyway, this movie was about this horrific man with razors for fingers and he haunted his victims while they dreamed. Then, the moment they felt safe, he attacked them, ripping them to a blended goop of ground-up burgers of flesh and blood. He wore a striped sweater and his face was covered in scars from what appeared to be bad burns. He scared me to my core. When the movie was over, I felt like I had been electrocuted—my bones tingled and were stiff.

Conifer was so nonchalant about it, like we had not just witnessed the most horrifying movie ever made. Without much talking, she rolled over to fall asleep. There was no way I could sleep after this super-scary movie. What if the terrifying man came into my dreams? Because I was such a vivid dreamer, it scared me even more and everything about me refused to fall asleep. Conifer, on the other hand, had absolutely no problem with sleeping.

I was shaking in fear under the covers of our sleeping bag, slumber party arrangement on the living room floor, paralyzed in fear. I was afraid to move, breathe, or relax. In the deathly stillness I heard noises coming from the kitchen. It sounded like someone was coming toward us very slowly. *Swish, swish … swish, swish … swish, swish* …. Then I saw a shadow growing on the wall—a bald man exactly like the man from the movie. His outstretched hands held something as he came closer and closer. I wanted to scream but was too afraid I would get yelled at by Conifer's mother and she would send me home and I would never, ever be allowed to come back. I glanced at Conifer, sleeping. Why couldn't I do that? It was too much for me—seeing her so peaceful while this monster was coming to attack us. I couldn't take it anymore.

"Conifer! Wake up!" I shook her.

She rolled over, still asleep.

"Conifer, he's coming to get us!" I shook her harder.

I heard the shuffles swishing and swishing closer and closer.

"Conifer, get up! LOOK!" The sound of my voice rose.

Conifer sat up and wiped her eyes. "What is it? Where?"

"Behind you."

Conifer peered into the kitchen and saw the huge, scary shadow, and lay back down, mumbling, "It's just Poppy. Go back to sleep."

"Huh?" I looked again and now could clearly make out the shrinking form of Poppy going back into his garage. I did feel a huge sense of relief that I wouldn't be turned into shredded meat. Still, I remained unsettled.

"I'm scared! Why did you show me that scary movie? I'm too scared to fall asleep and then start dreaming. That guy's gonna get me and kill me, I know it!"

"It was a movie, Holly. It's not real. Nothing to be scared of."

"I can't help it. … I'm scared."

She turned over to look at me. She must have seen the pure terror smeared all over my face, and felt bad. She smiled and called me silly.

"You're silly," I replied.

"You're a silly billy." She'd one-upped me as she stood to go use the bathroom.

"Oh, yeah? Well, you're a silly willy billy!" I double-upped her.

"Shhh," she said as I followed her, not wanting to be alone.

I zipped my lips and faced myself in the bathroom mirror. My hair looked ridiculous. On top of not having any bangs, the back of my hair sprouted up and around in all kinds of craziness. I flared my nostrils and made myself look even uglier, and then stared at Conifer, who had stopped near me. She burst out laughing at the hideousness of my head. She looked in the mirror and made ugly faces too, and we made silly noises to go with our ugliness. She poked at my nose, then I poked at her face, and before I knew it we were wrestling again all over the living room floor—until her mother came in, wearing curlers wrapped in a nightcap, a small nightshirt, and *big* white underpants.

She waved her finger around, saying, "That's it, I've had it up to here! With you, you, and you! And I'm not going to take it anymore!" She placed her finger on her forehead sideways indicating *where she had had it up to.*

We instantly stopped our assaults for an instant; the moment she turned to leave we burst out laughing, repeating, *"That's it, I've had it up to here! With you, you, and you! And I'm not going to take it anymore!"* We mimicked her finger gesture and said this over and over, and each time we sounded more and more ridiculous.

After I caught my breath from laughing so hard, I said, "Hey! Did you notice she yelled at three people?"

Conifer thought briefly. "What are you talking about?"

"She said, 'I've had it with you, you, and you.' I'm one you, you're the other you, who was the third you?"

The living room became silent for a minute and we searched around for invisible spirits as the chills invaded our skin. We saw nothing, yet felt something … something.

CHAPTER 18
NEW KIDS

New kids don't know how good they have it. Since all the other kids were used to everyone, when a new kid shows up, everyone gets all excited. I knew I was. There was a new girl and a new boy today. Her name was Begonia Barley and his name was Kale Collard.

Kale Collard was—how do I put this?—something about him drew me to him. I kind of wanted to stare at him … *a lot*. The clothes he wore seemed a little on the rough side. However, his clear blue eyes next to his sun-blazed skin had me feeling weird. While Coriander was telling me about his plans to get back to The Children's Horrible House, my attention and eyes lingered on someone else.

Kale seemed like the quiet type, and I wasn't as outgoing as my father so I wasn't sure if I would ever get to know him on my own.

"Are you even listening?" Coriander asked. He followed the direction of my eyes. "What are you looking at? Please don't tell me you like him."

"Huh? Like? Eww …. No, please …." I tried to sound convincing.

"I heard he was expelled from public school and that's why he's here," Coriander said.

I knew he was trying to warn me. So Kale *was* rough and tough. I knew it. My eyes must have glazed over.

"Stay away from him, Holly. Do you hear me?"

"I don't tell you who to talk to, do I?" I didn't like being told what to do, especially from my friends; at the same time, I appreciated his concern.

"Just trust me," he said as he shook his head, clearly disappointed in my interest.

Instead of getting to know the new boy, I had no trepidation when it came time to meet the new girl. After recess, Conifer and I approached her in the hallway.

"Hi, I'm Holly, and this is my friend, Conifer."

Conifer waved and said, "Hi, what's your name?"

"Begonia, but my friends call me Bug."

"Bug?" I said.

"Yeah, my mom said when I was a baby, my eyes were so big that I looked like a bug." She giggled a little.

Begonia had a unique look to her. She had pretty, dark skin and brown wavy hair that became lighter and curlier the higher it grew from her head. Begonia Barley was cool and she liked to laugh a lot. She liked rap music and she could even dance. I could not dance. During recess, some kids had gathered in a circle and took turns dancing on some cardboard while some move-making music was coming from a beatbox. I wished I could dance too. Some people's bodies moved with music in a way my tomboyish body could never do … at least not in public.

After school, Begonia's mom and my mom stood, talking to one another. My dad had to stay late tutoring, so my mom picked me up. Our moms seemed to like each other right away. They laughed and talked about church, groceries, and other boring adult stuff.

"Hey, Begonia, you want to go to a Primrose meeting with me?" I asked.

"Yes," she replied. "What's that?"

"Oh, it's a girls' troop meeting where we learn about different things, earn badges, plus we sell flowers, chocolates, and stuff. I don't know … stuff like that. Wanna come?"

She interrupted her mom and said, "Hey, Betula, I want to go to a Primrose meeting with Holly."

Betula? If I was right in my assumption, Begonia had called her mother by her first name *and* she didn't ask her for permission to go to the Primrose meeting, she kind of told her mother, which was not something I could do to mine—or at least I had never tried, anyway. She probably couldn't, either, I skeptically thought. Her mom was probably not going to let her go now, for being so sassy.

"Okay, Bug. First let me finish speaking with Mrs. Spinatsch, okay?"

Bug? Who was that? Oh yeah, I remembered now. Begonia and her big buggy eyes. … Why was her mother asking her daughter for permission? How was this possible? I was waiting for her mother to say something or paddle her. Incredibly, nothing happened.

Begonia was allowed to come with me to the Primrose meeting, after all. Begonia was a lot of fun even though she was kind of a brat. She had all the coolest clothes, music, and toys. Her toys weren't dumb dolls or Barbies; they were four-wheelers and big tractor tires you could fit inside. She lived in a three-story house that had a great view of a wide lake—and she had a pool. We lived on opposite sides of town, yet we played together almost every weekend. Our time was even more fun when Conifer came over too.

When we spent the night at Begonia's house, her mother made us chocolate chip pancakes which tasted better than any other pancake I have ever eaten. When she came to my house, we swayed on my tire swing, pretending to be astronauts launching into outer space. We explored my entire neighborhood, which wasn't exactly a neighborhood as much as it was a hilltop with a dash of homes. Behind our home was a large stream that had smaller fresh water streams pouring into it along its path, with beautiful plants that bordered the waterway. Around forty cement steps led to an estuary filled with overgrown flowering plants and towering climbing trees, like the forest in *Stars Wars* inhabited by Ewoks.

One afternoon we were walking around in the mud, gathering pinecones and interesting leaves, when she asked me about Coriander.

"What about him?"

"I think he's cute."

Of course Coriander was cute, but he was my friend and I didn't see him in that way.

"Do you think he likes me too?"

"I don't know." I shrugged.

"Can you ask him for me?"

Hmm. I wasn't sure how to answer this. I had never been asked to be a matchmaker before. Plus, for some reason, I felt this protective instinct for Coriander. Maybe this was the same thing he felt when I was looking at Kale Collard. Kale … my brain and/or heart turned to mush and started beating irregularly.

"Well?" She tapped her foot in impatience.

"I don't know."

"You don't know if you can ask a simple question?"

Begonia was used to getting her way, and I had seen the way she acted when she didn't, so I didn't want to disappoint her.

"I can ask, but …"

CHAPTER 19

Over at THE CHILDREN'S HORRIBLE HOUSE

The fire smoldered in the gigantic fireplace beneath the portrait of Hawthorne North Star. The reflecting light made the picture appear ablaze. If this had been the first time anyone had seen it, it might look sinister.

Seated under the flickering-flame candelabras, Clover and the PP twins swallowed the less than desirable assortment of foods they had been forced to consume.

"I have a plan," Clover told Staniel and Danley as they poked at their lunch in the dining hall.

"Yeah?" the twins asked.

"Yeah. Together we are going to finish what we started."

Staniel and Danley scanned the room to see if Miss Shapen was on patrol. There she stood, right beside the huge garbage can … inspecting it for any waste.

"Okay, I'll eat whatever you don't want to finish," Staniel offered while tugging on Clover's pudding.

"And I'll finish what he doesn't want," Danley grabbed the dish too.

"I'm not talkin' about food, you guys." Clover took back her pudding and placed it in her tray.

"So we can't finish your food?"

"Um, yes, you guys can finish my food, but I'm not talkin' about food; I'm talkin' about the treasure," Clover said, and whispered the last part.

"What about Holly and Coriander?" Staniel asked.

"We are goin' to do it for them," Clover said.

"What's the plan?" Danley asked.

"We're goin' to find that treasure!" Clover exclaimed.

"That's a good plan," the twins said as they rolled their eyes.

"I know," Clover said, pretending to know what her next step was. "I thought of it all by myself."

"I'll take that," Staniel said, and grabbed for Clover's pudding at the same time as Danley.

"No, not my puddin'! You can have these green beans." Clover blocked their oncoming pudding extraction while passing them her vegetable.

"Oh, man. I don't want those," Danley said with a sigh.

"I'll take 'em," Staniel said. He seized the bowl and gobbled the beans as Clover slurped her pudding while plotting their plan.

CHAPTER 20
JUNIPER'S MISSING

After Begonia left, I went to the kitchen and was stunned to see something I had never witnessed before. My dad was crying. My mom arched over his back as he sobbed. I didn't know what to do. My dad was in charge of everything. He never, ever, ever cried. I heard them speaking to one another. The only thing I could make out from their exchange was Juniper this, Juniper that, something Juniper. *What happened to Juniper*?

Entering the kitchen, I asked in a soft voice, "What happened to Juniper?"

My parents' faces clouded into the saddest expressions I had ever seen. My dad sat in a chair facing away from me, yet I could see his profile in anguish. My mother held his glasses and his head with her other hand. Her chin dimpled in sorrow. There was no joy or happiness remaining in her eyes, only serious concern. They had a hard time finding the words to offer to me; even so, my mom bravely uttered, "Juniper is gone."

"Gone? Gone where?" Hickory and Cashew ran in, wondering the same thing.

"She left—or rather, she's been taken away."

What was happening? First Filbert, now Juniper? *Maybe* she took Filbert with her to keep her company. I asked, "Is that what happened to Filbert? Did she take him with her, too?"

"No. She was staying with her friend, Luna, at her house; then we found out she left with her boyfriend, Hyperion, Luna's brother."

"Hyperion?" I knew Luna—kind of. I hardly knew her brother. How could she know him so well if I barely knew him?

"Did he kidnap her?" Hickory asked, and sauntered toward the phone, ready to dial.

"No, she went with him on her own."

"How do you know she went on her own?" I asked.

"Luna gave us this note when we went over to pick up Juniper. It was time for her to come home from the band/trumpet camp—where they were supposed to be …"

My mom handed me a wrinkled piece of paper which read:

Dear Mom and Dad,
I had to go get Holly.
Please understand.
I will be back.
Love,
Juniper

"Get Holly?" I looked up from the note.

She said, "Yes, but you're here." My mother sank onto the chair near Dad.

"I am. … So why isn't she here?" I asked, wanting to solve this horrible situation.

"I wish we knew, honey," my mom said as a new wave of grief hit my father.

"How do you know she went with Hyperion?" I asked.

"We don't. Luna said the two of them went somewhere together, supposedly looking for you, and have not come back. Luna assured us Juniper would be safe with Hyperion and he seemed pleasant when we met him those few times …" My mom's words trailed off.

"Where did she go?" I asked again, thinking if I kept on asking the same question, I would get an answer I liked better.

"We don't know."

"Oh," was all I had to say as my dad's form crumpled into my mom's belly.

I wondered if my parents were this upset when I was gone. They didn't even seem to notice I had been gone or that I had come back. Then something occurred to me ….

CHAPTER 21

THE CHILDREN'S HORRIBLE HOUSE

Several weeks later, Sirius was working in her office when Major Whoopins knocked at her door, escorting a girl who was older than most of the other kids brought here.

"Whom do we have here?" Sirius asked in her most demeaning voice.

"Dis girl say she lookin' fo' her sista," Major Whoopins stated.

"Her sister?"

"Holly Spinatsch, Miss Pankins."

"Holly, Holly, Holly Spinatsch .... Oh ... yes, Holly?"

Sirius knew exactly who Holly Spinatsch was. The little short-haired girl who always seemed to find Sirius in her less than best state. Even though Sirius knew who Holly was, she never imagined coming face-to-face with a relative of hers. Briefly stunned, Sirius scrutinized the features of the girl in front of her. Standing an average height, with pecan-colored hair and clear cerulean eyes, this girl was personable in her appearance, most opposite of Holly's less dignified approach. Holly resembled a young boy. However, there was a remnant of relation Sirius found behind the girl's eyes. Most apparent, this sibling of Holly Spinatsch was a ripe young woman who probably was unaware of her natural prettiness. Something dawned on the director: she had seen this girl before … here … a few years back.

After allowing Director Pankins to study her a few moments and without waiting to be spoken to first, Juniper said, "My sister was taken here and she's been gone a terribly long time, and I became worried so I went looking for her. I thought she was here, judging by the bus that picked her up from our home. But I can't find her here, either … and now I'm scared."

"Hmm … scared, are you? You should be familiar with this place." Director Pankins looked Juniper in the eye directly as Juniper held her gaze. "We don't usually have repeat visits."

"I promise I will leave as soon as I find my sister," Juniper said in a shaky yet brave voice.

Director Pankins stalled and plodded around her office trying to weigh her options on how to proceed. "Didn't you tell her, Major Whoopins?"

Major Whoopins wasn't sure what the director meant and felt himself get warm in embarrassment. He did not know what to say. His uniform suddenly seemed to be made of unbreathable fabric, constricting his breathing, and if he could turn colors, he would have been beet red. He wasn't sure what to do—if he was or wasn't supposed to inform this girl of Holly's whereabouts—so like he had always done in the past, he left all the talking to the boss.

"No, ma'am."

"Good."

"Tell me what? Where's my sister? Is she okay?" Juniper began to panic. She felt responsible for putting Holly on the dreadful bus, and couldn't stand thinking about what might have happened to her.

"Oh, yes! She's perfectly fine. Right, Major Whoopins?"

"Without a doubt," he said.

"Can I see her?"

"Yes, of course," she said in a very persuasive voice. "First, make yourself comfortable. It will be a while." Director Pankins walked back over to stand in front of Juniper. Her glare softened as she gazed into Juniper's eyes. "My, aren't you a pretty young woman. Major Whoopins, wouldn't you say?"

Major Whoopins once again felt warm. He didn't like being put on the spot. He cast his head down and nodded.

"And your name is, again?" Sirius Pankins asked with a kind smile.

Juniper studied the face of the beautiful woman in front of her and became mesmerized. Getting a wonderful compliment from such a sophisticated lady disarmed her and she felt flattered.

"Juniper," she said, and smiled sweetly and curtsied.

"Yes, now I remember," the director said, keeping up her pretense of ignorance. "What a lovely name. Major Whoopins, show Juniper to Holly's bunk. I'm sure she will feel comfortable there."

While Major Whoopins escorted Juniper to her accommodations, Sirius Pankins rubbed her hands together in excitement. What could be better? Perhaps this Juniper might be naughty like her sister and could lead her to the treasure.

CHAPTER 22

THE BEST GIFT EVER

Even though Juniper had been absent from home a lot, the house seemed emptier than ever. I hated not having my Juniper home. She stood as the barrier between Ginger and me. Ginger acted a little different now. She seemed nicer-ish, and I was thankful. I was riding my bike around the driveway one day, working on my wheelies and bunny hops, when Basil came to the house. I pedaled my bike after his car. He emerged, holding a big box topped with an oversized bow. I followed him inside the front door of our house. The gift was huge. It had to be something good to be enclosed in such a big box. Of course it was for Ginger. Regardless, I was especially excited to see what was inside. Whatever it was, moved, and I couldn't wait for

Ginger to open it. I stood staring at it, wishing I had X-ray vision or laser beams for eyes so I could open it "accidentally."

"GINGER!" I yelled as I ran toward the stairs. "GINGER!"

"WHAAAAT?" Ginger's muffled voice echoed from behind her door.

"Basil's here and he has a present for you. Hurry up!"

She took her time as I paced back and forth, apologizing to Basil for her rudeness. Eventually, like some debutante, Ginger descended the stairs, holding her cat, Sugar Snap, in her arms.

"Come on! Open it!" I said while scampering around the big box, barely able to control my excitement. It had to be something amazing!

"Hold your horses," she said.

She set Sugar Snap on the floor. Sugar Snap went to cleaning herself as soon as she was free.

Basil gave Ginger a kiss, and said, "I hope this makes you feel better."

"What is it?" Ginger asked.

"You'll have to open it to find out." Basil nodded toward the box.

"Open it! Open it!" I cheered as my hands flapped around like a crazy duck.

Ginger carefully opened the paper … as slowly … as possible … trying to preserve it, for some dumb reason. Her deliberations were killing me! Now was not the time for neatness. I stood in front of the gift, willing her to hurry, while a sloth had apparently taken over her movements. *UGgggH!*

As soon as she broke open the box, the cutest little puppy popped out, promptly knocked me over, and licked every inch of my face, and I loved it. I lay there giggling like a baby baboon until the dog found something new to investigate.

My eyes turned into gleeful saucers filled with delight. I had never seen a puppy dog like him before. He was going to be big! His fur coloring matched the sand of the seashore, but his eyes didn't even match one another. One was ice blue, the other, soft brown, and both appeared equally sweet. He acted extremely excited to see me—until he spotted Sugar Snap, and he became stiff—barely able to hold himself back from a sniff inspection. He lifted his nose to get a whiff from afar. His front legs dropped in front of him while his butt was hiked up in the air. The only thing that moved was his tail, which wagged his whole backside. The cat sat still on her butt, with one leg hoisted in the air, frozen between her cleansing licks. The puppy's tail abruptly stopped wagging, and the two animals stood still as statues, waiting for the other to make the first move. It was a standoff.

With the tiniest of movements, the cat sprang from her stillness and her hair spiked to full alert. Her body arched. Then, after the smallest twitch, she ran into the living room and you can probably guess the dog followed in hot pursuit. The chaos that ensued was all you could imagine—pillows tossed, blankets flung, couches trampled, lamps broken, etcetera.

"What in the world?" Mom said, when my parents approached, wondering what the heck was going on.

Well before Hickory came into the living room, we could hear him by his noises. As he stepped into the room, Sugar Snap ran into his legs. Instinctively, Hickory scooped the cat into his arms while she thrashed in life-threatening survival mode and grabbed onto Hickory's leg with her death-grip claws. Hickory grabbed Sugar Snap by the scruff of her neck, trying to loosen her hold, and she swung around and bit Hickory between his thumb and index finger.

"OWWWW!" Hickory howled as he tried to pry the cat's jaws and claws off his hand. Without much thought, Hickory shook the cat off his arm and kicked it away. Sugar Snap grunted at the assault.

Ginger yelled even louder, "Hickory! Don't kick my cat!"

"Your cat bit me!"

Ginger was too upset, watching her beloved Sugar Snap get tossed like a football. Of course, like all cats, Sugar Snap landed on her feet and ran for cover. I had seen her take even greater falls and get back up. I was absolutely sure she was okay, even though it still bothered me to see her get punted. I saw Hickory's wound and it wasn't a little bite. The bloody gash was pretty deep. When you get hurt, sometimes reflexes make you react to things without thinking. My mom took Hickory to dress his wound while Ginger ran after her cat.

After all the pandemonium, I found the puppy sitting with his head on top of his front paws, switching his focus from one eye to the other, like he knew he had behaved badly.

When my dad came back into the room, he asked, "Who's this?"

The dog practically crawled as low as he could while panting his apologies to him and offered my dad his head to pet.

"Aren't you quite the naughty fella?" My dad's knobby fingers scampered around atop the puppy's head.

"He's a fella full of mischief, it seems," my mom said after bandaging Hickory and putting her living room back together.

"I like that name," I said.

"What name?" Basil asked.

"Falafel. He's a fella full of mischief."

"Falafel?" They all said at once, sort of.

The puppy sat and looked at us, and then gave an attempt at a bark which turned into the faintest, cutest howl.

We laughed as we circled Falafel, giving him loving pats. I had hearts in my eyes when I stared at him and the feeling definitely seemed mutual. Falafel scampered over closer to me with his tail wagging him and formed himself into a bun shape, getting as close to me as possible. When I petted him, he rolled onto his back, hoping I'd scratch his belly. While I did, his one leg shook like it was trying to start a motorcycle.

I decided even though Falafel was technically Ginger's gift, he was *my* dog, and I think everyone agreed, even Ginger. Sometimes pets pick their owner and I had no objection.

I brought him outside and we chased each other till dinnertime. I devoured my supper, eager to go play with Falafel until bedtime. When I took my bath, I snuck him in and we covered ourselves in bubbles. He tried to snap at them as they floated away. I put some extra soap on him and lathered him up good. I made little spikes of soapy fur all along his back. All I could think about was how much fun Falafel and I would have from now on.

I was really missing Juniper and, for some reason, having Falafel helped me cope. He didn't say much, yet somehow he knew when I needed comforting. After I dried him off with a towel, with his sweet mismatched eyes, he looked into mine and communicated with a little puppy lick on my nose to accentuate his compassion. And nothing, besides having Juniper home too, could make me feel better.

We played together every day throughout the day. With Falafel, my life filled with abundance and I couldn't wait to see him when I woke in the morning or when I came home from school. Falafel came hardwired on how to play without being too rough. He was always extra gentle when it came to our wrestling, and I respected his sweetness. I would never hurt him.

Day after day, he grew in leaps and bounds into a respectable adolescent dog. I loved to practice soccer with him too. He ran fast after the ball and brought it back for me to kick it again. My favorite was when we raced around the driveway on my bike. I pretended we were in a big motocross race. Even though he was much faster than me, Falafel always let me win, coming to my side while I fiercely pedaled. He scampered alongside, looking at me with his tongue lolling around out one side of his smiling mouth. He followed me everywhere I went, with no need for a leash. Falafel could always be found by my side, being my best friend … and guardian, when necessary.

CHAPTER 23

THE CHILDREN'S HORRIBLE HOUSE LUNCH IN FRENCH

The long aisle in the center of the chamber was flanked with rows of bunk beds and at the far end, near the only window, sat Holly's old bunk. Juniper sat alone on her freshly made bed when a cute girl with dark brown braids tightly plaited on her head and skin the color of syrup glided toward her with a big bright smile. Instead of the coveralls all the other kids were forced to wear, this girl wore a long-sleeved, white nightgown that reached all the way to the wooden floor. She appeared to float above her invisible feet. At the sight of her, Juniper was reminded of a magical woodland fairy. As the girl came closer, Juniper saw that her eyes could barely open. Peering closer, Juniper discovered that the girl's eye sockets were windows into a blue universe of another distant world. The peculiar girl plopped onto the bed beside Juniper and crossed her hands in her lap.

"You lonely?" the girl asked while looking into the distance.

Juniper exhaled and said sadly, "I am."

The girl sighed. "I could tell."

Juniper and the girl sat silently and took in each other's company, exchanging energy. The comfort between them was immediate and Juniper responded to it.

"I came here hoping to find my sister; oddly, she's not here, and now I don't know if I should stay or try to get back home."

"I think you'd better stay."

"Why?"

"Well …" the girl's face turned, her gaze wandering around the room, and then she focused on Juniper and said, "It's 'cause I'll miss you."

Juniper smiled at the sweetness of the girl's gesture. "But you don't even know me," Juniper said, unsure if she was speaking accurately.

"Oh." She snapped her tongue. "Sorry about that. I'm Day-je-nay, but it's spelled Déjeuner."

Juniper paused a moment, thinking about the girl's name and what it might mean, while Déjeuner patiently waited for Juniper's introduction.

"Oh, I'm Juniper. Wow… Day-je-nay … that's a … a … beautiful name."

"I know. It means *lunch* in French," she said with a shrug.

Juniper smiled and let out a little giggle.

"Now we know each other," Déjeuner said as they shook hands.

"Yes, we do."

"So, now that we are friends, I can already tell we'll be the bestest friends and I never want you to leave, okay?" Déjeuner said this while two deep dimples formed on each of her cheeks as she smiled brightly.

Juniper agreed. Déjeuner offered Juniper her pinky, and Juniper hooked her pinky around hers in a swift swing. They both fell back on Juniper's bed with their pinkies still looped together. Even though they had just met, for both of them an instant comfort dwelled within their newfound friendship.

"What are you going to do today?" Déjeuner asked.

"Sit here, I guess."

"Boring. Let's go outside."

"And do what?"

"I don't know yet; when we find it, we'll know … kind of like when I found you, I knew you would be my best friend."

Juniper smiled. "Okay, let's go."

Déjeuner held Juniper's arm, letting Juniper lead her around. As they strolled, Déjeuner filled Juniper in on all the information she had gathered about The Children's Horrible House in the short time she had been here. They went downstairs and outside to the big field where a lot of the other kids played different games on the one weekly free day they were given. They continued past a game of four-square and then passed a group of girls playing a much more intricate game of pat-a-cake. A lot of the kids stopped playing and stared when they approached; not one offered to include them in the fun. The children weren't looking at Juniper as much as inspecting Déjeuner, when Juniper realized something was uncommon about her new friend.

Juniper led her away from everyone and found a nice shady spot beneath a handsome sprawling oak tree.

"What a nice day. I'm glad we're outside." Déjeuner gracefully sat, without exposing her legs or feet. Her gown seemed to cover something that wasn't there.

Juniper saw the blueness of the big sky and the puffiness of the clouds through the bright green leaves of the tree. With the breeze warm and the air fresh, Juniper took in an abundant, grateful breath. She regarded Déjeuner and watched as her face was pointed up and her eyes became filled with the picturesque reflections above her. Juniper had never seen such scenic, unique eyes.

"Can you see?" Juniper asked as a blue-and-black butterfly fluttered around.

In an instant, Déjeuner lifted her palm and the butterfly landed within it.

"I see what I need to see," Déjeuner replied, with a sweet smile as she held the exceptional winged creature up to her face.

Juniper was stunned. A butterfly—a remarkable and noteworthy blue butterfly—had never landed in her own palm, and she couldn't agree more with Déjeuner, saying, "Yes, yes, I see that you do."

CHAPTER 24

B.O.G.O.s

After school, instead of going home, my mom took us all to buy new shoes. Ginger was going to be modeling some wedding gowns for the local women's club, plus Cashew and Hickory went through shoes proficiently. My mom always shopped for the bargains, so Shoe Bazaar was our source for those BOGOs. I had my eyes peeled for one certain pair of sneakers. I walked along the aisles, weaving through a throng of black and brown bleakness when two shades of pink caught my eye. There they lay within a black-and-blueberry shoe box. Pink and raspberry Pro Wingerz with two straps of Velcro … waiting for me to crackle them open.

I searched for my size. I had an unusually large foot for not being fully grown, yet I still had the smallest feet in my family. For some strange reason, I liked my big feet; I thought they made me look cool. These shoes would make my feet look even bigger! I found my large size, ripped out the wad of packing paper, and slipped on the cutoff pantyhose. My foot slid in perfectly, just like Cinderella's—only this was no useless glass slipper. My other foot wanted to get in too, so I pushed it into the left shoe and closed the Velcro straps. Boy, did these shoes look great! I lifted my toes up and around, searching for any discomfort. Nope, they fit perfectly. I bet they could go really fast too. I ran to my mom and showed them to her.

"Mom, here's the shoes I want. Can I get them?"

"I don't think so, honey. No one else can find a pair they like, and if we can't do the BOGO, it's a no go."

I wasn't prepared for this scenario. Why would a mom bring a child to a store, knowing the child needed something and then not get the child what she needed?

I was about to fall on the ground in misery, when Cashew saved the day.

"Mom, I found a pair. These are the shoes I need," Cashew said, holding out a pair of white tennis shoes.

"I can't find a thing here," Ginger said, as if the BOGO store wasn't good enough for her. "I'll have Basil take me to the department store."

"My shoes still have a couple of months left in them, Mom," Hickory chimed in. "I'll get new ones then."

Hickory had only two pairs of everything. Two pairs of pants, two pairs of underwear, two shirts, and two pairs of shoes. Any more, and Hickory wouldn't know what to do with the extras.

"Okay. Holly and Cashew, take your shoes up to the register."

"Can I wear mine home?" I asked, too excited to take them off.

"You'll have to ask the lady," my mom said as she signaled for us to make our way to the front of the store.

* * *

I ran to the car. "Look how fast I can go," I called to my mom as I bolted through the parking lot.

"You're not any faster than you were before, you hemorrhoidal liver spot," Ginger called out.

I knew she was trying to burst my bubble. "Uh-huh! Am so!" I ran again, this time doing some flashy zigging and zagging, exhibiting my speed while she rolled her eyes.

CHAPTER 25

NEIGHBORS

When we arrived home from the store, Mr. Painintheas, our Greek neighbor, waited for us with Falafel on a leash. He yelled at us to keep our dog from chasing his chickens.

"He's-a going to-a catch-a one, one-a day and, I-a tell-a you, he will-a kill it and then I will-a kill-a him! Do you-a understand-a what I'm-a saying?" he told us kids.

Falafel always stayed close when we were home; however, when were out, he must have become lonely or curious and did some explorative walks. As soon as Mr. Painintheas let him off the leash, Falafel bounded over to us and sat like the good dog he was. He gazed at me and breathed heavily in and out of his mouth. I bent over and took his head in my hands and gave him a good scruffy petting.

"Yes, sir," we all replied, respecting our elders while actually wanting to say something else.

Mr. Painintheas had never been my favorite neighbor, even though, for the most part, he kept to himself. He had a daughter,

Thisbe, whom I occasionally played with. But overall, I found his company uncomfortable. In his front yard, he had a huge boat. We called it the arc, and for as long as I can remember, the boat never felt any water beneath its hull. He had chickens and other kinds of animals. He told us the next-door neighbor, Mr. Tortolini, complained about Falafel chasing his peacocks, too. Falafel only wanted to have fun. I knew in my heart of hearts he would never harm one of those fowl.

Mr. Tortolini had a yard filled with all kinds of animals, mostly chickens and guinea hens. Recently he had acquired some peacocks and they sounded much like the ones from The Children's Horrible House. Mr. Tortolini was a sculptor and he had all kinds of questionable sculptures placed in different arrangements around his property. On some of my explorations, I snuck over to his place and stared at the stone formations and wondered how he thought up each piece.

We all placated Mr. Painintheas by telling him we would keep Falafel from chasing his chickens. I knew it would be difficult. The neighbors at the absolute end of the road always fed Falafel and Falafel went through Mr. Tortolini's and Mr. Painintheas' property to go to the last house, belonging to Mr. and Mrs. Skaditsky. The Skaditskys loved Falafel, too. I think they secretly wanted him to be theirs. Since their daughter worked at a veterinary clinic, she took Falafel in for all his shots and regular upkeep simply because he was such a likable dog. So, in return, we kind of shared Falafel with the Skaditskys.

CHAPTER 26

Back at THE CHILDREN'S HORRIBLE HOUSE

Months passed, and Sirius Pankins inertly sat at a standstill. She was no closer to finding the treasure this day than the night she found those meddling kids poking around in her father's tomb.

The new children who had come after Holly and Coriander's departure were evidently not as curious as them. Sirius had tried to entice a few; sadly, they were horribly good, always staying in their beds, never snooping, and behaving far too well to belong here—unless they were even more sneaky than she knew. She decided to keep a closer eye on those twins and Clover. They had to be up to something.

Sirius preferred the feisty kids, the ones with moxie, the ones who found trouble … leading to treasure. This new batch of brats were about as exciting as Mormons on Sunday. Juniper had been a disillusion; the only thing she seemed interested in were the boys—who found her irresistible.

Intimidating these kids was almost no fun. It was too easy. Sirius found herself bored and listless, looking at herself in the mirror. What she saw no longer resembled the young girl with golden, raging fire in her eyes. The flames, tired from being smothered in exhaustion or perhaps boredom, gave off little vibrancy. What she saw did not make her happy. She was losing hope.

After berating herself for a while, she felt like giving up and merely existing with no purpose until she died. … Maybe she could thrive at being boring and learn to knit or crochet? The thought went in and right back out. All this searching and researching, to come up empty-handed became draining.

She readied for bed even though she hadn't even eaten her dinner. She had no appetite. As she lay, about to relax, she heard her name. Not Sirius, she heard the name Saffron … delivered by the wind, coming from the cracked window to the right of her sizeable deluxe bed. The unidentified source whispered so faintly she thought she'd possibly imagined it. She went to the window and opened it fully. The air spilled into her chamber, refreshing it with a cool nighttime scent … which reminded her of the night she ran away from here many years ago. The branches from the substantial oak tree brushed the outside wall of her chamber. The leaves and limbs made a scratching effect which sounded whispery. Something called out to her, and she had a feeling it wasn't the branches. She couldn't ignore it anymore. Like picking up on a much desired scent, she followed the summoning feeling outside.

In the quiet of the glowing garden, Sirius meandered along the paths of flowering bushes, listening for her name. The sky was dark and the night-blooming plants slowly began to start their show. She was letting her fingers dangle as they played with the higher shrubs.

She wandered over to the fragrant flowers and took in their scent. She ducked under the arbor bursting with blooms of passionflowers as they tickled the top of her head.

Being within the walls of this comforting place helped Sirius connect with her parents. She thought about who she used to be when her mother was still with her. Remembering the look on her father's face when she told him of her plans to build this garden, shame overcame her in knowing her plans had been to deceive him. She wished she could crawl back into his always welcoming lap and feel his doting love. Her senses recalled the small bursts of breath in her hair as her father read special picture books to her as a child.

Her mother also gave her ample amounts of affection, and as Sirius reflected on her childhood, she ached to feel her mother's comforting embrace again. She loved feeling her mother's hand twirling through her long dark hair. Many times her mother held her and hugged her while telling her about her destiny. Sirius remembered her father saying the same things after her mother had gone; at the time she couldn't stand to hear what she believed to be lies.

She cried out, "Why? Why did you leave me?" She wasn't sure if she was yelling at her mother or father or both. She fell onto her knees next to the mausoleum and thought of her father's face that used to anger her; now she wished she could tell him how sorry she was. If only she could go back in time and undo all the pain she had caused so many people, especially her father. It hurt knowing she was the source of his death and possibly the reason for her mother leaving. Slowly a void overcome her, leaving her open and blank, as if she'd slipped into another dimension or consciousness, when out of nowhere her mother's spirit appeared, surrounded in clouds. Or at least that's what it appeared to be at first. The cloud moved in a way clouds don't normally move. A fluttering motion which appeared to be a stop-motion movie exploded into a dispersal of pale yellow butterflies. The cloud opened and her mother was floating within the kaleidoscope of the delicate winged creatures. Sirius could clearly see her mother right in front of her. She thought she must be hallucinating; at this point she did not care.

Being able to see her mother under any circumstance was preferable to the pain in the absence of her. Her mother sang a song Sirius had never heard before, though it felt strangely familiar. Sings-in-the-Meadow chanted in her native language, but the tune was much more typical of an old song from Sirius' father's family hymnal. Somehow she was able to translate and understand the words.

Fly, fly, fly like a butterfly
gliding on wings of the wind,
Never having to hide deep inside your cocoon—once again.
Look, look, look all around you,
Your chains are gone.
you've been set free;
Safely resting with me once again.

The song brought tears to Sirius' eyes. She tried to sing along; doing so made her even more emotional. She fought back the heat and boiling tears when the cloud of butterflies surrounded her with their wings flicking her face, arms, and legs. An essence held her in a warming embrace. The hug enveloped Sirius' entire being and she felt a healing force that permeated her hardened outer shell. The wings of the butterflies brushed her cheeks and wiped her tears, leaving her face luminescent under their touch. In this moment, Sirius knew her mother had not forsaken her and Sings-in-the-Meadow was still with her, even if only in spirit.

Slowly the flutter lifted, leaving Sirius alone yet not forlorn. With new tears of joy streaming down her cheeks, Sirius' eyesight was shrouded in leftover visions of the encounter with her mother. Sirius opened her eyes; as she found some focus she saw the peacocks staring at her while waking in the garden. One by one and then at once, they cried out, startling her, as she sat up.

"Shhhhh," she whispered to the birds.

They weren't as obedient as the rest of her staff.

CHAPTER 27

SOMEONE'S SLEEPING IN HOLLY'S BED

Clover and the twins hid behind the mausoleum, witnessing Director Pankins under her spell. They saw her in a way they had never known her to behave. What they witnessed was like watching someone under hypnosis. She seemed like she was in a trance. Clover felt a strange pity for the director and wanted to comfort her, even if only telepathically. She knew if the director found them, the three of them would be in big trouble, so they had to keep quiet. When the peacocks surrounded the director, at first they only stood around her, inspecting … then a twitch from the bushes behind them set them off and they began to cry out, waking Miss Pankins from her semi-slumber.

"What was all that about?" Danley asked, after the director fled.

"Who knows? But guess what?" Clover said.

"What?" Staniel asked.

"Someone new is sleepin' in Holly's bunk," she said.

"Who is it?" asked Danley.

"I don't know, but she looks like a teenager, an older teenager."

"When did she get here?"

"A few days ago, I guess. I have a feelin' about her," Clover said, as her face squinted, reflecting her hunch.

"What's your feeling?"

"She knows somethin'."

"Wow … she knows something! You're really amazing. Are you a psychic or something?" Staniel sarcastically joked.

"I must be," Clover replied.

"Hey, guess what?" Danley said.

Staniel said, "What?"

"I know something too."

"What?" his twin said.

"I know you guys are a couple of worms," Danley said. He huffed as he turned to go.

"Speak for yourself," Staniel said.

Clover couldn't help herself, and said, "I think I can speak for all of us when I say, we're goin' to be worm food if we don't get outta here."

CHAPTER 28
NEW SNEAKS

On Friday I strutted into school, sure everyone would notice my new pink sneakers. I was ready for a race too, if anyone decided to challenge me. I walked remarkably upright, with confidence to spread around. On the way to each of my classes I sneaked peeks at my sneakers every other step. Boy, was I proud. I felt bad for some of the other kids who wore their much more ordinary-looking shoes to school even though they could wear sneakers or any other shoes they chose on Fridays.

For some reason, no one congratulated me on my new shoes. No one even noticed or cared about my prized pink sneakers. And when I saw Conifer, she had on a *new*—even cooler pair of turquoise-blue sneakers! They had three black stripes and this cool zigzag pattern to them. Conifer had a substantially smaller foot and those new turquoise-blue sneakers fit her feet perfectly. I inspected my larger pink sneakers and suddenly saw my clownish big feet and no longer thought the big-foot thing looked so cool.

Phooey.

I opened my lunch box and took inventory of its contents. At least my lunch was still going to be tasty. Begonia sat with us at lunch, too. She did not have a lunch box or bagged lunch; her mom brought her a Fun Bun Meal from McDoodle's. My mom never, ever even drove us to McDoodle's, much less brought something from a fast-food restaurant for me to eat at school. Begonia's french fries smelled so good. I wanted to ask her for one and she could tell.

She held it up and wafted it around for us to get an even better sense of its taste, and said, "Mine," as she chomped on it.

Conifer sat quietly eating her "rabbis." I decided not to bring up the topic of my new shoes to Conifer. She noticed them anyway.

"Did you get some new sneakers?" Conifer asked after her final slurp.

"Yeah … you too?"

"Yeah."

"Do they make you run really fast?" I asked as I snuck a closer look at her treads.

"I don't know. Guess, no faster than before."

"So your new sneakers are just as fast as your old pink ones?"

"Guess so." She shrugged.

"Wanna race later?" I asked, eager to test out the speed of my pink ones against her blue ones.

"Those shoes look like you bought them at a gross BOGO

place. I refuse to shop at those stores," Begonia said, diminishing the integrity of my new shoes as mere bargains.

Ouch.

"Hey, it's a three-day weekend. You want to come spend the night at my house this weekend?" Begonia said.

Not to dwell on the insult she delivered to my sneakers, I responded, "Yes!"

"I was asking Conifer, not you."

Ouch, again.

I promptly felt ugly and poor. In reality, I already knew I was ugly; however, until now, didn't know I was poor as well. My bangs were butchered. I had big feet, thick glasses, and I probably stunk too. Who would want to be friends with someone as ugly and as poor as me? I did have *some* friends … like Staniel, Danley, Clover, and Coriander, who didn't seem to care how ugly or poor I was. Then I remembered the stings of friendship from my time at The Children's Horrible House with Cherry and Clover. I never became immune to the hurt.

I may be ugly, but my sneakers were awesome even if they were a bargain BOGO. If Begonia didn't think my shoes were as special as I did, that wouldn't keep me from liking them for myself.

Later, in PE, Coach Cotton moved me from goalie to forward. I decided to really test what these shoes could do. I ran in the mix today and with my new sneakers, I was sure to impress. Most of all, I hoped to impress Kale Collard. He played on the opposing team, so he would be able to see me in action. Being that he was rough and tough, I wanted to show him how rough and tough I was, so I was giving it my all. I was kicking and hustling the ball from the best of them. Coriander even seemed surprised by my skills.

When Kale had the ball, I knew I had to get it from him in order to really surprise him. When I did, my shoe that was a tad too big tripped him and he fell to the ground, which by all accounts was funny—seeing him trip. So I laughed … Anyone—even Kale Collard—seen tripping is funny, right? But when I laughed, he balled his fist and punched me square in the left temple.

Ouch … literally.

Funny thing is the punch itself did not hurt. The stunned feeling that overcame my consciousness fogged my brain from performing any function other than standing there with a goofy expression.

When out of the dust, I heard, "HEY! You can't punch my friend!" and I watched my little, brown, puffy-haired Begonia, a.k.a. Bug, punch Kale Collard in his face. And her fist-to-chin contact was impressive.

He returned with a punch to her head.

And she socked him again.

Then he punched her again.

Coach Cotton dropped his balls, blew his whistle, and ran over to Kale. He put him in a head lock, keeping him from throwing any more punches. I don't know what took Coach so long to respond, but I think everyone stood a while in shock at the scene.

Coriander ran over to me and asked if I was okay, while I watched Begonia holding her face as Conifer comforted her.

I had never been punched before, and I had never had anyone stick up for me like that, either. Begonia took two hits—punches—for me. In that moment, Begonia had my friendship forever—no matter what.

Camellia, who hadn't been as much of a nuisance as I thought, ran over to Kale as he was being escorted away by Coach Cotton. She grabbed his free arm and gave him a nasty Indian burn. Kale pulled away from Coach to clutch the arm under attack while she persisted savagely burning his arm. She turned to me and nodded, like she had my back, too. I decided she might not be so bad after all, and gave her an appreciative lopsided smile.

CHAPTER 29
THE DEAD BIRD

When I was ready for school the next day, I bounced down the stairs and saw everyone outside the back door, peering under the picnic table. Ginger held her mouth like she was witnessing something horrifying. Based on her expression, I wasn't sure I wanted to see what was under there. Ginger turned her head in my direction.

"What is it?" I asked.

"One of Mr. Tortolini's peacocks is dead. It died under the picnic table," Cashew said as I watched Falafel going around the table, sniffing the poor bird's body.

"Oh, no! How?" I asked.

Ginger only shrugged her shoulders.

After everyone had examined the fallen fowl, including Falafel, Hickory set off to find a shovel to give the bird a proper burial.

"Don't you think we should tell Mr. Tortolini?" I asked.

Cashew shook his head. "Not if you want Falafel to live."

"What does the peacock have to do with Falafel?"

"He'll probably assume Falafel killed it."

"Falafel would never hurt even a kitten and we have plenty of those," I argued.

I dropped to one knee to give Falafel a big hug and pat on the head. He licked my face in agreement.

"We know Falafel didn't do it," Cashew said. "Look, the bird doesn't have a single scratch … not even a feather out of place. It looks like the poor peacock just came over here and died."

"Yeah," I said, "Falafel's a good dog. He'd never go and hurt a thing … 'specially this peacock."

I stared at the peacock, in its reflecting iridescent blues, greens, and other colors I could not name—none could give justice to their beauty. The peacocks at The Children's Horrible House were pure white, and this one was multicolored but predominantly blue. Both versions of the bird were beautiful and majestic; no one could say which was more beautiful. I felt incredibly sad for this fallen angelic creature. Falafel howled a mournful tune for the poor bird, showing his respects. I kneeled down to hug him as he continued his eulogy.

Throughout the school day, the image of the poor peacock kept popping into my head. When I saw Coriander, I told him about my morning and he seemed to be taking it all in; the mention of peacocks brought his mind back to the glowing garden.

"Remember how they cried for help?" he asked.

"Yes! At first I thought a baby or a ghost was crying!"

"I know. I think Hawthorne North Star put them there to act as an alarm."

"Hey, they worked!"

"Yeah. Did you notice the peacocks cried out even when we weren't in the garden?"

"Yeah, you're right, they did."

"Someone must have been in the garden those nights, too."

"It was probably Miss Judge. Remember how we saw her one night in a flowing white nightgown?" I asked.

"You mean the night we were taken away?"

"No, the first night we went into the garden. … Oh, wait, you weren't with us then," I said as my brows scrunched.

"I helped you out of the garden one night, remember?"

"Yes! It was the same night, only we saw what we thought was a ghost wearing the same nightgown Miss Judge wore the night we were taken away."

Coriander seemed confused, so I decided I should explain the whole story. "We saw what appeared to be a ghost wearing a white flowing gown, going into the garden, so Staniel, Danley, Clover, and I followed it. As you know, we became lost trying to leave the garden, until you came in. Didn't you see the ghost?"

"No, I never saw it. You say the ghost was wearing the same gown Miss Judge wore when she and Director Pankins had us taken away?"

"I can't be positive, but I think so."

Coriander put an index finger to his lips and squinted his eyes.

"Where are you going in your thoughts?" I asked, sure his pondering headed somewhere exciting.

"Everywhere," he answered.

Phooey.

CHAPTER 30

THE CHILDREN'S HORRIBLE HOUSE

Speaking of the rest of Director Pankins' staff, the librarian had been noticeably silent. Sirius went to look for her in the library. The director came to the double doors and stopped, focusing her eyes on the circular cross symbols in the grill that protected the glass. They had always been there, as well as other places throughout the house. She remembered seeing the symbol at the gate outside of the glowing garden. Nothing in this house was coincidental; it had to mean something important. Sirius mentally kicked herself for not paying more attention to the wisdom her parents tried to bequeath to her.

She opened the doors and expected to find Miss Judge reading or organizing some books. For some reason, she was never around when Sirius or anyone else came into the library.

The director roamed through the aisles and wandered into the nooks and spaces where someone might be hiding. She found no one. She walked to the back south wall and scanned it for anything and anyone. She shook her head as she became overwhelmed with a flood of books from floor to ceiling. Little did she know that finding the right book was discovering something sacred. Volumes and volumes of thick books with their spines showing outward seemed to hold millions of meaningless words—all except for one. A skinny, flimsy thing held together with leather string stood out of place.

Sirius lifted it and as she did, a hidden door creaked and opened to a darkened, barely lit chamber with a spiral staircase in the middle. Sirius went inside and found some personal items that must belong to the librarian. Sirius climbed the swirling stairs. At the top, several landings intersected with each other and led to a central observatory open to the sky.

"Hello?" Sirius called and instantly heard a gasp.

"What are you doing in here?"

"I could ask you the same thing," Sirius retorted.

"We've already had a conversation like this." Willow, the librarian, put a hand on her hip and would have rolled her eyes if she hadn't been so sophisticated.

"Not necessarily. In fact, I don't remember finishing that talk." Sirius peered around and saw from here, that Willow had a conspicuously good view of the library. Willow had to have seen her come in. Sirius glanced over at Willow and then saw the upper observatory, which appeared to have seen some recent action.

"What's going on up there?" Sirius motioned with her head.

Willow glanced behind her and saw her unfinished business evident, as various calculating tools resettled from use. She realized it would be futile to be coy, so she answered her somewhat truthfully. "That's difficult to answer without boring you to death."

"I know all about boredom," Sirius said, and sighed. "It

consumes my current daily life. Really, I've nothing better to do than to be even more bored by you. Please do enlighten me. I'm already interested."

Willow couldn't tell if Sirius was being sarcastic or truthful. She was guarded, but Sirius gave Willow her full attention … so Willow thought perhaps she was serious. Willow hoped to have this interaction over as quickly as possible so she could get back to her work.

"I'm right in the middle of figuring out something I don't have an answer to right now. So really, I have no definite answer for you. However, if you want to stay and watch, you might learn something," Willow said as a distinctly unique-looking cat gracefully jumped onto the high platform directly under the observatory.

He was a large creature with slightly crossed blue eyes, of a wheat color with cinnamon-colored tips, and a long, purposeful, striped tail to match. The cat snaked around obstacles, prowling his way toward the sisters. When he jumped up next to Willow he raised his front paws and wrapped them around Willow's neck and brushed himself on her chin. Willow offered him her forehead and scratched his back. For a moment, she closed her eyes, nonverbally communicating with her purring pet.

Sirius was intrigued. She had never had an animal of her own. Willow saw Sirius watching her and her cat, and felt uncomfortable. "You get down now, Copper," she said, and placed him on the floor while the cat continued his attentions by weaving his lithe body between Willow's legs.

"Copper? He does look reminiscent of the metal," Sirius observed.

"His full name is Copernicus, after the great astronomer."

"Do you miss him?" Sirius blurted, even slightly shocking herself.

"Copernicus? No, I've never met him. It would be difficult, considering he's been dead for over four hundred years." Willow had a feeling this wasn't what Sirius meant.

"No, not him. I'm-I'm speaking … of our father." It felt strange to include Willow in the small family she once knew.

Willow shrugged and went to arrange the notes on her desk. "I never knew him. I was given away soon after I was born."

Sirius knew Willow had not been given away to just anyone, but she allowed Willow to feel sorry for herself.

"Did you find your grandparents to be cruel or unwelcoming?"

Willow stood there trying to figure out how deep this conversation could go, and decided to not let it get much further. "To answer your question … I miss my whole family, and yes, of what little I knew of my father, I do miss him," Willow said with more emotion than she had planned.

Witnessing Willow's emotions caused the walls Sirius had constructed to keep her mission on track to suddenly feel compromised.

"Hmm." Sirius looked at Willow, not trying to intimidate her, but more to search for some semblance of their father in her face. Willow must have taken a lot of her facial features from her mother. Her structure resembled her sire.

The cat finally gave up his quest for attention and made himself comfortable on what had to be his kitty throne, a small-scale daybed covered in lush fur, topped with a canopy holding a small mobile of the solar system for the cat to bat when feeling frisky. His accommodations were situated in a nook next to a large wooden desk with odd pieces of paper and tools surrounding it.

"I see you are making charts and measurements. Anything I can assist with?" Sirius believed she was no match for Willow's wealth of accumulated knowledge. That didn't stop her from pretending to know more than she actually did.

"I'm not sure. See, I've been making some calculations based on celestial mechanics, with formulas for positional planetary predictions, and what I'm finding is remarkable. It's almost unbelievable." Willow felt strange, sharing this information with Sirius, but wanted to test a possible relationship with the only blood relative Willow knew to be alive.

Before Willow ever came to live at The Children's Horrible House, she had learned the rest of her siblings had passed exceptionally early in life. Her oldest brother died from pneumonia and the other two died together traveling from England where their boarding school was located.

Sirius nodded and tried to look like she was thinking, and she *was* thinking—just not about all the science stuff. She realized this observatory must be where Willow actually stayed—lived. A comfortable-looking bed and a fully equipped bathroom jutted off one of the landings. The overall industrial setting appeared comforted by Willow's decorative feminine touches. Sirius peeked into the bedroom and found a painting of the original Hawthorne Star Family. It must have been before Willow had been born, because her mother, Hyacinth, was alive and well in the rendering. Captured on the wall was a great picture of a beautiful family … before their devastation.

"Do you always let yourself into other people's rooms?"

Sirius ignored Willow's question and stated, "I've never seen this picture before."

"That's because it's mine."

Sirius shrugged at her explanation as they stood together in front of the portrait, seeing a family that existed wholly before the two of them were born. Willow's mother had died while giving birth to her. Willow inadvertently had been responsible for the disaster that fell upon this once complete family. If it weren't for her birth, her mother would still be alive and her family would still be intact—with no Saffron … i.e., Sirius Pankins … no Children's Horrible House.

Sirius saw something else. She saw a family who caused her mother, Sings-in-the-Meadow, to leave her. Willow's brothers and sisters believed Sirius' mother was pursuing the Star family fortune, when nothing could be further from the truth. Money and wealth meant nothing to Sings-in-the-Meadow. The same could not be said for Sirius. Even though looking at this family caused them pain and anguish in different ways, something made them hold on to shreds of the familiar.

"You favor your mother," Sirius noted.

"You, as well."

"You knew my mother?" Sirius was taken aback.

"Not like you did, no. I did see her, and she was remarkable," Willow reluctantly yet truthfully admitted.

In this moment they turned, faced one another, looked into one another's being, and recognized the relation that should be their bond. Somehow, something, perhaps distrust or unforgivingness, kept them apart.

"I should get back to work." Willow went behind the safety of her own walls, and Sirius picked up on the disconnect.

"Oh, yes, if that's what you want to call it." Sirius instinctively tried to keep the upper hand. Her desire to know more caused her to put her superiority aside, and she extended a peace offering.

She said, "I'd like to learn more … more of what you're finding, mechanical calculating, whatever you're learning … Rather … I should say … well, the unbelievable things," Sirius said as she bent over to pet the cat who was curled into a cinnamon bun. "It wasn't as boring as I thought it would be."

Copernicus purred in response to the attention and opened himself up for further massage. Sirius found the animal to be undeniably adorable, and felt a tinge of jealousy over their obvious bond.

Willow watched Sirius pet *her* cat and saw the sincerity in the attention Sirius gave. Plus, by his interaction with Sirius, something felt hopeful.

"You might want to talk to Miss Guide, she's the real expert here," Willow said. "I talk with her a lot about my findings, and she has always been exceedingly helpful."

Sirius stood, put a small smile on her lips, and said, "Thank you, I will."

As she turned toward the spiral stairs to descend, Willow noticed Sirius' skirt askew. It was tucked into her waist, revealing the greater section of Sirius' butt.

"Miss Pankins! I can see your fanny," Willow called out.

Sirius stopped, looked behind her, and saw her skirt flipped up, exposing her backside. She quickly pulled it out and pushed it down, wondering how long she had been flashing everyone behind her. Without saying a word or looking back, she descended the dizzying stairs.

CHAPTER 31

ONE DAY, I PROMISE

"These beds aren't going to make themselves. Let's go, you lazy, good-for nothing, mess-making children," Miss Place called out. "I swear, these kids keep getting lazier and lazier," she mumbled as she paced the room.

Clover watched the new teenage girl making beds. The older girl had a younger girl acting as her shadow, moving at the same speed and with the same grace, helping her make beds. There was something strangely familiar about this new girl and Clover had to find out. After Clover finished making her bed, she sauntered over, pretending to assist the two girls with their bed.

"Have I met you before?" Clover asked as she tucked in some of Juniper's sheets.

"Oh, thank you," Juniper said, noticing Clover's aid. "I don't think so. … My name is Juniper Spinatsch. What's yours?"

A huge grin spread over Clover's face. "Spinatsch?" she asked.

Déjeuner stopped what she was doing to make sure her best

friend was not going to be mistreated.

Juniper was used to people finding her last name comical, and thought, *Okay, let's get this over with.*

"Spinatsch, like Holly Spinatsch?" Clover asked excitedly.

Juniper's guard dropped. "You know my sister?"

"Holly's your sista? Where is she?"

"I had hoped you or at least someone in this place might have that answer."

"We were all togetha' when she and Corianda were taken somewhere. We assumed back home, but now since you're here and she isn't, I'm even more confused."

Clover's grin faded to worry.

"I came here looking for her. I was responsible for her coming here in the first place." Juniper put her head down as guilt invaded her conscience.

"Hey, it's not your fault," Déjeuner interjected. "We are all here as a result of something we did. None of us are innocent."

Juniper thought about what she said and tried to not feel so bad; still, she felt responsible for her little sister.

One of the older boys strutted over to Juniper, practically ignoring Déjeuner's and Clover's presence. "Hey there, why don't you let me take care of these beds for you? You just relax."

Then another, shorter, boy came over and jostled the other one out of the way and offered his assistance. But the jostling became a little too rough. Miss Place called for mean old Mr. Meanor, who showed up and grabbed the two boys by the scruff of their coverall shirts and they were taken to THE DUNGEON.

"You can help me with mine," Clover said to them as they were being dragged away, but the two boys only had eyes for Juniper.

"Thanks, guys, but I can handle it." Juniper waved to the departing boys.

"Gosh!" Clover sighed.

"I know! They won't leave me alone," Juniper said in a huff.

"I neva' have that problem," Clover said, and shrugged.

"You will one day, I promise you."

"I won't!" Déjeuner put her hands on her hips and twirled around with a goofy expression on her face, making Juniper and Clover laugh.

"Less laughing, more bed making, girls," Miss Place said in her warning voice.

The three of them dutifully went back to work.

CHAPTER 32

TINSEL TREE ISLAND

Conifer couldn't spend the night with Begonia on the weekend, so Begonia decided to come over to my house instead. Begonia liked me, I guessed, but she *loved* Dookie and *especially* Falafel. Who wouldn't? He was such a good dog, way better than dumb ol' Filbert. I kind of hoped Filbert would never be found. Falafel was growing really big. The Skaditskys, those neighbors at the end of the road, fed him a lot. Even as he matured, Falafel never barked. When he heard a police or ambulance siren, he howled like the part wolf he was. His other influences appeared to be golden retriever or husky. Falafel followed Begonia and me around as we explored the stream-side woods beyond the steps from my backyard. We called it Tinsel Tree Island because there was a gigantic silver cedar tree that stood proudly in the center of it, and to me it smelled like Christmas which was right around the corner.

We stomped through the Tippy Toe Trail and pushed back moss as we advanced through the thick foliage on our way to the Tinsel Tree, which stood waiting our arrival.

"Did you know my house is haunted?" I asked in a spooky voice as we explored the mushy land.

"It is?" Begonia really perked up. I liked having her attention, so I took full advantage of it.

"Yeah. Supposedly, the man who built my parents' house way back in the 1800s was a doctor. His name was Dr. Genungal, the same name as the road I live on. He's the ghost—Dr. Genungal."

"How do you know it's him?" she asked.

" 'Cause of what the Boocowskins, the next-door neighbors, said. They said he haunts their place too. Apparently, when he was alive, he used their house as his doctor's office. He was a dentist and he used the tall tower with lots of windows on the east side of their house for good lighting."

"So why would he haunt your house and their house too?"

"I don't know. Do ghosts always make sense?"

"Guess not. How did he die?"

"No one really knows, but I heard his wife killed him because she became jealous of one of his nurses. Apparently, the wife suspected he was involved with his younger, pretty nurses and she killed him and the nurse in his office. After the murders, the wife came home and drowned herself in the fountain—now covered up in the front of my yard—'cause she didn't want to go to jail."

"Huh." She thought it over. "So, what have you seen?"

"Okay, so the lights often go dim with no explanation, and sometimes I hear a door slam and when I go check it out, no one is there. Plus, one time it looked like someone had dug themselves out from the place where the wife supposedly drowned. There were all these weird claw marks in the dirt."

"Maybe there is more than one ghost," she said after a ponderous pause. "Maybe the wife ghost haunts your house and maybe the doctor ghost haunts your neighbor's house."

"I never thought of that. What about the nurse? Maybe she's a ghost too, and they are all haunting the houses together."

"Hope they *all* leave us alone tonight," she said as a chill swept across her body.

"It's okay. We have Falafel to protect us," I said, patting him on his side while we toddled through the woods.

We had enough of all the spooky ghost talk and quickly redirected our focus from our make-believe haunted world to something much more pleasant. We pretended to be lost princesses. Not the boring, do-nothing princesses who waited for rescue, though. More like warrior princesses, princesses who could kick butt until help such as a big, strong movie star could arrive. And since I no longer had any room in my heart for Kale Collard, I filled that space with someone more appropriate, Superman.

Begonia and I played really well at our pretend games. At the bottom of the Tippy Toe Trail was the Tinsel Tree. The leaves and the bark were probably ordinary-looking to everyone else, but to us, everything about this tree was magical! It was taller than any other tree in the world, so tall it must scrape heaven's floors. The branches went all around the globe and everyone could meet anyone in the Tinsel Tree *if* you knew the secret code language. Begonia and I did, so we could access the tree.

"OOKA LAKA SEENA! OOKA LAKA SEENA!"

"PEEPA LAKA LOOKA! PEEPA LAKA LOOKA!"

We shouted our chants in unison in order for us to gain access to climb the tree.

"MELLA COLLO WELLE! MELLA COLLO WELLE!"

"TONSI COLLO WELLE! TONSI COLLO WELLE!"

The tree responded by saying those words to us. Since the tree couldn't actually speak, we said the words out loud for it, like we were speakers for the Tinsel Tree.

After climbing up and around, searching for the perfect branch, we settled in, ready to meet all of our imaginary friends. In the Tinsel Tree, Begonia and I met a lot of different people, like amazing, glamorous movie stars and famous musicians, and some stuffy geniuses who were perplexed by *our* brilliance. Model scouts looking for the *It* girl were always in the Tinsel Tree and we both happened to be perfect and everyone, absolutely everyone, loved us.

"Yes, dah-ling, it is so difficult to go out in public these days, with simply everyone wanting your attention," my character, named Swansea Sinclair, complained while my arms floated around in a glamorous gesture.

"Oh, to be normal!" Begonia's character, Xanadu, exclaimed while placing her hand on her forehead in dismay.

Lucky for us, we had a whole slew of movie stars and famous people to keep us company in the tree. They also understood the cost of fame. Within the magical branches of the Tinsel Tree, we were all we wanted to be, which was so much better than reality. So we stayed long into the dusk.

In the distance the trees, heavy with moss, swayed like ghost-filled clouds. The moon began its ascent as the overall spooky setting was enhanced by the soft howl of Falafel faithfully waiting for us at the base of the tree until we finished with our imaginary visits.

While climbing down, I thought about how glad I was for the three-day weekend. Now we had two whole nights to spend together.

CHAPTER 33

A TWO-MAN HOLE

The weather had been strange. It was getting closeer to winter yet still warm. Even though my house had air-conditioning, my dad refused to turn it on. I became used to it, for the most part. Begonia was more accustomed to the luxuries she had at her home.

"It's hot, Holly. Go turn on the AC," Begonia pleaded.

"I can't. I'll get in trouble."

"No, you won't. Go do it. *I'm dying*," she said in a dramatic tone.

I wanted her to be comfortable, but when we weren't having loads of fun, she complained. Realizing she wouldn't be satisfied until I did as she beckoned, I reluctantly stood and snuck downstairs.

Each step acknowledged my foot with a squeaking creak, no matter how lightly I stepped. Normally those thirteen steps proved easy to travel up and down. At this time of night, they seemed to growl louder and louder in my dissent. My ears became so sensitive I could hear even the tiniest movement in the house. I felt like I was back at The Children's Horrible House, exploring the echoing halls in the cover of darkness. Uh-oh … the hairs on my arm rose and I became stiff. Someone was watching me. Was it the ghost of Dr.

Genungal? I imagined his scaly corpse floating out of his grave and coming at me like a zombie, ready to feast on my flesh. I went a little faster, hoping to elude the decomposing dead man.

I finally made it to the bottom stair, and Falafel raised his head off the laundry room rug. He twisted his head, wondering what I was doing here at this hour and why I looked like I had seen a ghost.

"It's okay, Falafel. It's just me. You can go back to bed." I rubbed the top of his head, setting him back at ease.

I continued on my nighttime journey to the air-conditioner dial located all the way in the living room. Through the foyer, I was able to make up some time. I stepped up into the living room and spotted the round thermostat. I stalked over to it to see the temperature setting; since the room was dark, I couldn't read the numbers. I knew if I shifted it to the left, the air-conditioner was supposed to come on. The moment I was about to set my hand on the dial, I heard a deep, terrifying voice right behind me, say, "Holly, what are you doing?"

I sprang about five hundred feet off the ground, pulling muscles which cramped in response to the unidentified horrifying voice. Okay, maybe I didn't jump that high and I hopped more like five hundred centimeters, but my whole body screamed, including my mouth, until I turned and saw that the deep, terrifying voice belonged to my dad—which wasn't all that terrifying after all. Because I was being sneaky, his unexpected deep voice scared the poo-poo out of me! I covered my mouth in order to hold back any more rogue screams and bent over, trying to compose myself. How did he get here so quickly and so silently? He was in bed, I thought. When I came down the stairs earlier, I saw my parents' door closed and it was only shut if they both were in there.

"Um … Begonia's hot, Dad," I said, and ran back up to my room before I could get in trouble.

Begonia was sound asleep when I came back—of course. My shoulders slumped in exasperation—all that for nothing. I lay back down. It took me a while to fall asleep—after being scared half to death. And with the slight snoring sounds coming from Begonia's nasals, finding sleep was even more difficult. My brain kept thinking. Then I became aware of the thinking my brain was doing and wondered why most of the time I thought without thinking about thinking. My thoughts eventually became exhaustive and over time, I found the rest that had been hiding from me.

The next day, Begonia woke bright and early, ready for action. I rubbed my eyes—eyes which did not want to open, and after a lot of Begonia's prodding, I slowly awoke. The morning overflowed with activities Begonia declared to be fulfilled. After we ate our mystery breakfast she'd concocted out of flour, water, eggs, and green food dye, we baked some questionable pies. Due to our skills in the kitchen being subpar, we decided to start our more advanced construction, our outdoor activities. First on the agenda was building a pool. Because my father insisted on living in heat, we found a way where we could, you know, cool off before bed—in a pool.

I had always wanted a pool and I imagined what ours might look like. I conjured a bright blue pool with wavy, slippery slides and a high, bouncy diving board where I could perform many acrobatic tricks. I imagined myself jumping and twisting and impressing everyone who witnessed my talent. Unfortunately, this one wasn't going to be one of those big, oversized pools with slides and a diving board. Sadly, we didn't have the time or the cash for such construction. We had a very strict budget of zero dollars, so our pool would be more of a two-man hole in the ground for us to take a dip in before bed.

We worked all day, digging and digging somewhat of a circular shape, about two-and-a-half feet deep. We stood with our shovels still in hand as Cashew came out to inspect our work. He didn't seem too disappointed; in fact, he even gave us the clever idea to line the pool with a plastic tarp. We took his genius idea and then followed it with holding the tarp in place with various bricks, buckets, and other heavy objects. Dusk descended as we filled the pool with water from the hose. We were so excited to plunge into our hand-dug pool, we could hardly wait for the water to get to the invisible fill line.

With the moon rising from the eastern sky, we slipped into our underclothes, too impatient to put on our swimsuits, and slipped delicately into our new fresh, hose-filled pool. The coolness of the water enveloped our bodies and at once we transformed into sea nymphs under a starlit sky. We pretended to speak in our sea creature language, which sounded more like dying dolphins, but we knew what we said. We flapped around in the super-small shallow pit in pure bliss, exultant in our accomplishment.

"Pretty good, huh?" I proudly boasted.

"Not too shabby," Begonia said.

A rustling of leaves caused us both to turn and see a dark shape slinking around. What was *that*? If my hair wasn't soaked, it would have stuck out like I had been electrocuted. We both caught a bit of a fright right before we realized Sugar Snap was only burying her doo-doo.

Though we were relieved, the small scare must have conjured a thought for Begonia. She said, "I heard some screaming last night."

"Screaming?" I asked.

"Do you think it was the ghost of Dr. Genungal's nurse?"

"Oh, no. Those screams came from me."

"Did you see the ghost?" she asked, with her eyes bugging out, and now I finally understood why her mom called her "Bug."

"No, worse … I saw my dad, who busted me as I tried to turn down the air-conditioning for someone who didn't seem to have any trouble falling asleep after all."

"Oh." She bowed her head and sheepishly giggled.

Cashew came out to see us in our new, luxurious dipping pond.

"Do you love it?" he asked.

"Yes!" we both replied.

"Are the bricks holding the tarp in place?"

"Think so." I nodded and patted one of the bricks to demonstrate its durability.

"Good," he said, and turned to go back inside.

From our pool, I could see my mom getting supper ready. Ginger helped her as Hickory fluttered around the kitchen taking samples of food from their preparations like a hummingbird. Even though I couldn't hear him, I knew Hickory was singing something. My dad sat in his spot reading his old-car magazine. The amber light made everything look so ideal from this point of view.

"I wish I had brothers and sisters like you," Begonia said out of the dark silence.

I didn't think she wanted anything I had. I thought she had everything *I* could ever want.

"Really?"

"Yeah, you have a great family, Holly. I wish I wasn't an only child sometimes."

I hadn't thought about what it would feel like to be an only child. I had always had my brothers and sisters around. Being the youngest, I never knew my family dynamic other than what it became the moment I was born. I wonder how Hickory felt each time a new brother or sister was added to his world. I heard he had cried when they told him my mom was pregnant with me; luckily, he never seemed to hold it against me the way Ginger did. She had been the baby for six years before I came and stole her coveted position. Even though she pretended to not like me, I always loved her; actually, I idolized Ginger. She was the smartest of us all, and beyond beautiful. I never even attempted to compete with her; I knew it was a lost cause. She would and could always win and I was happy knowing my sister, Ginger, was a winner. I think that's why Basil always bought her things … he knew she was way too good for him. Ginger kept him around due to his super-cool sports car and the smart timing of his gifts, which made me think about Falafel.

"Hey, I haven't seen Falafel all day," I said, with a strange feeling creeping into my gut.

"I haven't seen him either," Begonia said.

"That's not like him. Normally he's with us wherever we go."

"I know. That is strange. Watching us dig all day probably wasn't how he wanted to spend his time."

"He's probably with the neighbors, eating his extra meals." I hoped.

"Yeah, probably." Begonia tried to sound upbeat.

CHAPTER 34

The Children's Horrible House

What Sirius didn't realize was someone was waiting for her in her office. The gentleman was walking around the room, inspecting the contents atop Sirius' desk. He held the nameplate and emitted a smidgen of air in an annoyed "Pfff." He sat in the high-backed leather chair and swiveled around. Looking above, he saw the portrait of Sings-in-the-Meadow and the young child, Saffron. Hawthorne North Star, his esteemed employer, had treasured this stunning portrait. He had found Hawthorne staring into this portrait many times. The man regarded the child, Saffron, noting she was such a delightful creature when she was small.

He remembered her dancing around the house, wearing the black moccasins her mother had made for her. Saffron always wanted to play hide-and-seek with him. He'd be busy with his day-to-day comings and goings and as he came around a corner, Saffron popped out and said, "Boo!"—then ran into his arms and let him hug her for a minute before wanting to be found "Again! Again!" Saffron was an adorable child, and when her mother left, it was difficult for him to see the changes she went through and not be able to comfort her the way only a mother's embrace could.

From the opposite side of the room the door opened, and the man swiveled around. Sirius' gasp gave away her obvious shock and, at once, her face flashed back to the sweet child he was so fond of—many years ago.

When she lifted her hands to her mouth to gasp, she fainted. Her body crumpled to the floor as if it had been emptied of its blood and other life-sustaining contents.

The man rushed to her side and held her head, saying, "Saffron, Saffron, come back! Can you hear me?"

Her body lay limp in his hands, her breath unsteady. Instinctively he felt her neck, looking for a pulse. Her vitals seemed strong—just like Saffron—even though the color had vanished from her face and lips.

"Saffron, Saffron, wake up!"

He scanned the room, searching for something to help her become conscious again. He had almost set her head back down when he heard a soft "Reed?" Her voice was as unsteady as her breathing.

"Yes, Saffron, it is I."

She looked into his eyes and then scanned his face in disbelief. Reed Trustworthy was her father's faithful butler and the original director of The Hawthorne House for Children, the name this place had been called before she took it over … before she became Sirius.

"Reed Trustworthy! Is it you? Is it really you? I … I thought you were …" She couldn't even form the last word before a tear dripped from her cheek.

"Dead?" Reed said.

She wiped her eyes and replied, "Well, yes …."

"Surprise," he said in a most uncelebratory fashion.

After Sirius realized she had fainted, she blushed at her frailty. Reed helped her up and escorted her to her chair while she tried to regain her composure.

"I see you've made some changes to the place."

"Um, yes, you could say so." She detected some changes Reed had gone through as well. For one, he had aged, though not in a less proficient way. He actually seemed stronger and more capable than before.

"I know what you've been up to," he said.

After the initial shock, her eyes readjusted to her more guarded, calculating position, trying to understand the meaning of his words and the reason for his sudden reappearance.

He examined many objects and pictures while Sirius watched him without saying much. Casually he sashayed over to the high-powered telescope Sirius had pointed to the sky. He took a look within the scope and adjusted the lens.

"I'm here to help," he lightly said. Turning around, he gave her a warm smile, walked over to her and gave her a light kiss on her forehead before he opened the door to leave.

"I'll see myself to my room," he turned back and said before he stepped out of the doorway.

Sirius sat stunned, still utterly perplexed about what had happened. She wasn't sure if she was more surprised by the sudden reappearance of Reed Trustworthy or that she had fainted. Carefully, she stood and paced around her office. What was Reed Trustworthy up to? She couldn't believe he was actually alive. Now her identity was certain to be exposed. It had already, somewhat. And did it really matter? This was her rightful home, after all. For some reason, it felt like she was about to lose everything. Where did this shaky feeling come from? She stood at her window, looking out to everything and nothing at once … deep in thought. She casually squinted into her telescope almost by instinct. When she actually saw where the lens pointed, she was more than baffled.

CHAPTER 35
MOM FARTS

And just like that, winter was upon us. The air turned crisp as the season took hold. A whole week went by and Falafel was nowhere to be found. We talked to all the neighbors; they seemed either sympathetic or to have no knowledge about where he could be. Mr. Painintheas was never around for questioning, which made me suspicious. A few years back when I was playing at his house with his daughter, Thisbe, I remembered going into his bathroom. Hanging upside down from the shower rod were various empty animal skins—those poor woodland creatures. His whole house was dark and creepy and I never, ever went over there again.

I anxiously thought about all the losses our family had experienced. Ever since I came home from The Children's Horrible House, pets and people had been disappearing. What was going on? Were Filbert and Falafel taken to The Horrible Puppy Pound? Maybe Juniper had been taken to The Children's Horrible House.

I lay in bed trying to sleep, but all these hypothetical pestering scenarios kept infesting my head, causing me to be restless *again*. I tossed and turned, trying to find the sweet spot on my pillow that held my head and lulled it to sleep. I moved my eyeballs back and forth to tire them out. Slowly my head sank in, giving away its tension and eventually I must have found peace.

Before I knew it, morning came and with it my mother's singsongy voice rolled through the house.

"Gooooooood moooooooorning," she sang, and a couple seconds later I heard her sit on the toilet and let out the longest, loudest, different-pitched fart, amplified by the toilet bowl, ever.

"Oh! My tummy feels better," she let us all know.

I was awake *now*, for sure, and so was everyone else. I heard some scolding voices say, "MAH-uhM!" telling her moms were never, *ever* allowed to *fart*! Our scolding was useless, although an absolutely necessary reprimand.

We had to get ready for church. Church was the last place I wanted to go. I had to go, no matter what, so I went without too much trouble. We had started going to a new church and it happened to be at my school. During the week the giant sanctuary served as a gymnasium. On Sundays it became a loud, boisterous, music-filled hall. The coolest part about this church was Begonia's and Conifer's moms brought them here, too. This church had loud music that made people dance. Guitars, piano, flutes, drums, and tambourines jammed together to create a feet-stomping, body-twirling experience. Begonia's mom and my mom danced together in the aisle, embarrassing us to no end. My dad and siblings adhered to the quiet, more reserved singing while my mom was unstoppable.

"MAH-uhM! Stop dancing! You're embarrassing me," I said, and she turned to me for a minute, hoping to make me feel better … then the music took over and made her body scamper, scuttle, jump, twist, and clap, and I couldn't stop her, no matter how much I wished she would. I tried closing my eyes, and then pretended to be somewhere else or someone else, which proved to be futile.

Begonia caught me attempting to stop my mom from dancing and she signaled for me to look at her mom making a complete fool out of herself, too. She was doing what looked like a circular polka mixed with an original flare only she could do, and then we both started laughing.

Conifer's mom had more control over herself. She kept her swaying within her pew. Begonia and I both went and sat with Conifer, who was in the same pew as Melia, the smart know-it-all, speller extraordinaire.

After church was over, all four of our moms talked nonstop, so we naturally took advantage of this free time, joking with one another until we came to a more serious subject.

Begonia asked, "Have you found Falafel yet?"

"Who's Falafel?" Melia asked.

"My dog."

"He's missing?"

"Yeah, for about a week."

"That's too bad. I hope you find him."

I don't know how, but Melia had this way about her that made her seem much older than other kids our age.

"Thanks." I couldn't help become worried for him. Where was he? My expression must have matched my thoughts.

Melia's concern for me became apparent on her face as well.

"Maybe we should pray about it."

I wasn't sure if she was asking or telling. At this point, I was ready to do anything to find Falafel.

I had never prayed with my friends before. I usually saved those prayers for when I was about to take a test I had not studied for or if I really wanted something special for Christmas or something important like that. I looked over at Begonia and Conifer, who both shrugged and agreed to pray.

Melia clasped our hands and we formed a circle outside the pew. At first I felt extra self-conscious about everyone seeing us pray. I tuned in to the outside individual conversations and found none of them included us. When I tuned in to Melia'a prayer, without effort a radio signal reached the receiver. Melia prayed for Falafel to be found, for someone to lead us to him, and for God to keep him safe. I prayed too. I prayed for Juniper. I prayed she'd be safe and for her to come home quickly. I prayed for Falafel, my sweet, howling, one blue-eyed, one brown-eyed dog. I even said a tiny prayer for Filbert. I became lost in our prayer and found myself in a realm I didn't know existed—a place in between thoughts. A new yet familiar consciousness took over, until I opened my eyes and found us surrounded by the whole congregation muttering words in a language I could not understand. After the prayer concluded with an "Amen," I felt thankful to Melia for offering to pray for Falafel and it made me appreciate her in a way I hadn't before.

"You girls want to have Sunday dinner at our house?" my mother offered to all of us.

Melia had never been over before, unlike Conifer and Begonia, who had both been over many times. She looked at me, giving me a chance to invite her personally.

"Would you like to come to my house?"

Her mother, after some thought, gave her permission.

Begonia, Conifer, Melia, and I rode home in the back of my mom's Buick. And my dad took everyone else home in one of his loud, smelly, old cars everyone else seemed to drool over.

Our favorite song came on the radio and we sang and danced in our seats until we pulled into the driveway.

"Who's that?" Begonia asked.

I checked through the windshield. "That's Mr. Painintheas' daughter, Thisbe. She comes over once in a while. Her parents are divorced and her mom lives north of town."

"Why is she waiting here at the driveway?" Conifer asked.

"I have no idea."

Thisbe was sort of fun when she came to visit her dad; since those visits were so rare, I felt like I had to get to re-know her every time she came around.

After my mom parked the car, the four of us girls scuffed over toward Thisbe. She wore a strange outfit, as usual. She had on a red cape; under that, a one-piece purple bathing suit which didn't fit right, shiny red boots, and she held a shepherd's staff which was actually a gnarled, rotting stick. I think she was going for a superhero look; sadly, there was nothing *super* about this look except for her determination to wear it so boldly.

"Hi, Thisbe," I said.

"Hi. Are you missing a dog?"

I couldn't believe my ears! "Yes! Do you know where I can find him?"

"Yes. However, I'm not sure you're going to like it."

I did not like her tone, but she was prone to exaggeration.

"Where is he?"

"Well …"

Thisbe was acting coy, and my friends looked like they might shake her.

"Is he a big dog with yellowish-blondish-colored fur?" Thisbe asked.

"Yes! Where is he?" Now *I* was about to shake her.

"I think he's dead. Even I, Thisbe the Great, couldn't help him."

I think time stood still for more than a moment as the words she uttered slowly made their meanings understood.

"What? NO! It's not true! It's not true! You're lying, you … weirdo. *You're lying.*"

Thisbe flinched at my assault.

"Holly!" Melia said, scolding me, while my friends backed away, not knowing how to respond.

"What? She's lying! She has to be lying!"

"My dad saw his body floating in the stream, with a chunk of his side missing," Thisbe heartlessly said.

"Your dad probably killed him!"

"No, he said Mr. Tortolini killed him because your dog killed his peacock."

"Falafel didn't kill his peacock! It just died!"

The blood in my face burned my skin. I became so hot I ripped off my bunny hat and threw it on the ground. I was furious. How could this happen? Not Falafel … he couldn't be dead. We prayed! We prayed! … It must have been too late.

I ran away from everyone, up to my room, buried my face into my pillow, and cried. I cried so hard my head throbbed and my eyes became bloodshot. Snot smeared all over my face as my head pounded. I couldn't imagine a life without Falafel. He was the cutest, sweetest dog anyone could ever imagine, and he was mine. I kept hearing his soft howl as a new wave of grief overtook me.

My mother came into my room and pushed back my hair, trying to be of some comfort. She was, but the hurt I felt was unbearable.

The insides of my body had been taken out, blended, and then spit back inside in no particular order. My head felt like it might implode. Nothing made sense and I couldn't stop being sad.

Eventually my friends came into my room. Melia placed my bunny hat next to me on my bed. I'm sure they didn't know what to say or how to make me feel better, so they sat there quietly at first. I could hear Begonia sniffling, and Conifer cleared her throat every once in a while.

The four of us sat stunned, saddened in silence. What could we do?

Melia seemed to be the most coherent of us and she said, "We should have a funeral for Falafel."

It seemed sudden. At first no one knew how to respond, so everyone gathered themselves together.

"How?" Conifer asked.

"Do you have any pictures of him?" Melia asked me.

I was still sad, mad, and thinking of useless ways I could bring Falafel back, when I realized Melia's question was directed to me. I thought about it and answered "Yes" as I wiped my nose.

"Okay, show me where they are so we can make a collage."

I redirected my thoughts and found the basket of pictures. Hundreds of pictures of my family on various vacations lay piled, but I didn't have time to reminisce. I sifted and gathered all the pictures I had of Falafel, which weren't too many because he wasn't very old. Melia arranged them on pieces of construction paper and drew hearts around them. Begonia and Conifer each added little messages to Falafel. They also drew some wings on his back like he was a little puppy angel.

The Boocowskins, our next-door neighbors, heard about what

happened to Falafel. One of their younger sons made him a wooden cross, as he had done in the past for fallen woodland creatures that had died on his watch. Still, no one seemed to know for sure who was responsible for Falafel's death. I was pretty sure it was Mr. Painintheas. On the other hand, it could have been Mr. Tortolini. But Mr. Tortolini had always been so nice. I couldn't picture him killing Falafel.

My dad and brothers went and recovered Falafel's body so he could receive a proper burial. They wrapped him in a sheet. I could make out his form beneath it and it crushed me to see him so … not alive. The sun set and I shivered as the air cooled even more as Cashew dug the hole that had been the pool Begonia and I had dug, deeper. He had removed the tarp and dug to six feet and they carefully placed Falafel inside. After they finished filling in the dirt, Cashew marked the grave with the cross given by the Boocowskins. I placed our collage in front of the cross and stepped back, looking at the upturned ground which now held the body of my sweet, howling Falafel.

My tears started to overwhelm my head and soon they poured out from my eyes. I could hear my friends sniffling and wiping their faces, trying to keep it together.

My brothers and even Ginger gathered a bunch of wood, branches, and sticks, and lit a gigantic bonfire. The flames grew strong and reached higher than even Hickory, who stood so tall. Wafts of smoke slithered around and filled the air with its scent. Crackling and spitting out in small bursts, the fire paid homage with flares reaching into the night sky, sending signals to Falafel's soul, telling him we loved him. I hoped he could feel it as he hovered above us in doggie heaven.

Sitting around the fire, each one of us took a turn saying something about Falafel.

"The first moment I saw him, I knew he was going to be the best dog ever ..." I said, and then started to feel the emotions take over. Tears welled in my eyes and my chin quivered. I took a long breath, reached within myself, and found some courage to keep speaking and not fall apart. "He licked my face from top to bottom and he had the best puppy breath ever." I recalled the unique, sweet breath he panted, and then I crumbled as I cried into my hands. I felt Ginger's hand pat my back; I quickly turned and hugged her tightly, sobbing into her stomach.

Begonia said, "Um ... I remember the time we were walking through the Tippy Toe Trail to Tinsel Tree Island and um Falafel wouldn't let us go past him ... he blocked our way and we didn't know why he was doing that. We told him to move, but he stood there not letting us pass, and then Holly started to push him out of the way and then when she did, we saw a poisonous snake slithering across the path. We screamed and ran away. Falafel saved our lives that day. He had seen the snake and um he protected us." Begonia had managed her speech through a lot of hiccups and ums.

"I remember how he played fetch," my father said, "and he never seemed to have been trained. He came preprogrammed for fun. And you know, he always sat when everyone else sat, without being told. He was a good dog."

It made me glad to know even my father appreciated what a good dog Falafel had been.

"The whole time he was here, I don't think he ever pooped in the yard," Cashew said. "I mean Filbert, he left his poop piles in specific spots just so I would step in them, but I never, ever stepped in Falafel's poop."

Hickory, heartless as ever, offered: "That's 'cause he probably always pooped in Mr. Tortolini's or Mr. Painintheas' yard."

It seemed to lighten the mood.

"I never met Falafel," Melia said, "but I do know he's in a very special place right now, with God in heaven."

Ginger gave me a good squeeze, and I wiped my ever flowing tears.

"You hear what she said, Holly?" Ginger pushed me back, firmly holding onto my arms. She looked me in the eyes with her own tears spilling, and said, "He's in heaven now! And heaven is a marvelously great place! He's probably running around in meadows, playing with dragonflies and birds. He's probably eating rainbow ice cream and drinking glitter water. Now, doesn't it sound wonderful?" She sniffled and wiped her nose.

It did make me feel better knowing Falafel now lived in such a great place. I thought back to our prayers for Falafel and wondered why it turned out the way it did. I thought again … my prayers had been answered, although not how I expected. Falafel had been found and he was now safe. And Melia and Ginger had a lot to do with me knowing he was in a much better place.

We
You Falafel!!
FALAFEL
Best
Doggie
Ever!

CHAPTER 36

The Children's Horrible House

Sirius paced the length of her office, trapped in her own circular maze of thoughts. What was Reed Trustworthy, her father's butler, doing here? How was he still alive? It had been a number of years and there had been no hint at his vitality. Her relationship with him as a toddler had been warm; however, things cooled as she grew. Could she still trust him? He had always been so good and faithful to her father and seemed trustworthy … she laughed, thinking of the irony of his last name … Trustworthy.

There was something off in his demeanor today. She couldn't be sure. Her instincts told her to beware, especially after seeing where he had been looking through her telescope. The lens wasn't pointed to the sky with rivers of puffy clouds; it was focused on her father's tomb.

She scanned her office and felt something out of place, but couldn't tell what. She took a quick look out of her powerful telescope again. This time she searched for any heavenly signs to point her in the right direction. When she turned around to look at her desk, her eyes went to her nameplate that was supposed to be on her desk. It was missing. She found it poking out of the trash can. She strode over, picked it out, and put it back on her desk, knowing with certainty who put it there.

Sirius stormed from her office, ready to make a big accusation, when she saw Miss Guide walking across the hallway in the distance. Sirius called out, but saw Miss Guide had gone beyond the corner of the intersecting hallway. She increased her pace and rounded the corner, calling out again. This time Miss Guide heard her.

"Yes?" Miss Guide stopped even though she was evidently in a hurry.

Sirius felt strange asking. She hesitated and then decided to go forward with her request. "I wonder if I could speak with you about … um … well, astronomy." Sirius felt uncomfortable asking her subordinate for advice on any subject. But Sirius knew deep down she didn't know a whole lot about anything. She figured if she pretended really well, people might think she was smart.

"Actually, I'm heading into class right now. Why don't you come in and observe, and if you have more questions, you can ask after."

Sirius didn't like the thought of sitting through an entire class like some idiotic overgrown student; even so, she painfully accepted the invitation.

She had decided some time ago she must not be part of the horrible population of useless children. When she spotted Holly Spinatsch's older sister, Juniper, in the class, she became focused on her until the lesson grew somehow interesting.

"Astro*metry* … yes, you heard me correctly. Astrometry is a branch of astronomy which involves the tools used for precise measurements of the positions and movements of stars and other celestial bodies. The information gathered by astrometric measurements provides information on the kinematics and physical origin of our solar system and our galaxy, the Milky Way," Miss Guide said while showing a picture of a known point in outer space that would be used as a baseline for calculations of stellar positions.

Sirius wondered if this was what Willow was using for her calculations.

"Astrometry is linked to the history of star catalogues, which gave astronomers reference points for objects in the sky so they could track their movements." Miss Guide pointed to a picture of stars in outer space.

"Even though this seems, and it is a very advanced part of astronomy, everyday people like you and I can learn and understand astrometry. It can be dated all the way back to around 190 BC, when Hipparchus used the catalogue of his predecessors, Timocharis and Aristillus, to discover Earth's precession. In doing so, he also developed the brightness scale of the stars that we still use to this day."

With head scratching, nose picking, and deep stares into nothing, the children in the class seemed not as interested as Sirius. She wondered why she hadn't paid more attention to the available wisdom found here in her own home.

"Hipparchus compiled a catalogue with at least 850 stars and their positions. Hipparchus' successor, Ptolemy, included a catalogue of 1,022 stars in his work, the *Almagest*, giving their location, coordinates, and brightness."

Miss Guide thought she'd liven up her classroom by getting the kids involved. "Guess what instrument is used to make these determinations?"

No one raised their hand.

She pulled out a large, circular, bronzed-metallic object which resembled a clock, only with much more intricate detail. It had a dial on it and other uncentered circles. Sirius thought she had seen something similar to this in Willow's observatory. Straightaway, the whole class became interested.

"It's called an astrolabe. Does anyone know who else might use this instrument?"

A young boy who sat next to Juniper spoke out: "Um … sailors?"

"That's correct! Sailors use the stars for navigation. Isn't that amazing! To think, distant stars, lightyears away, help little seamen find their way to and fro around the world's vast oceans. I find it remarkable how dependent we are on our universe and yet how unaware we are of its presence surrounding us and how it impacts our lives. Some people say the stars even influence our individual behavior. … Who knows?"

Miss Guide rested at one corner of her desk in silent contemplation, before clapping once, getting herself back on course.

"It's interesting to think of … the same instruments that can guide you around our formidable oceans are the same ones used to explore and understand the infinite universe! Take a look at this … this is called a sextant."

From a hinged wooden box, she pulled out the most intricate-looking protractor ever.

"A sextant is a doubly reflecting navigational instrument used to measure the angle between any two visible objects. Sailors were able to find the angle between an astronomical object and the horizon. The angle, and the time it was measured, can then be used to calculate a position line on a nautical chart or an astronomical one."

Miss Guide demonstrated how to use the instrument. "First, in order to find your latitude, you should find the day's maximum angle between the sun and the horizon, and then write down that angle when the sun is at the maximum rise above the horizon. Then you look up your longitude in the tables for the current day." She held up the book of tables.

"Second, you record the time at your chronometer—oh, I almost forgot! A chronometer is an exceptionally precise clock. Then, when the sun reaches the day's maximum angle, that moment is your 'local noon.' To find your longitude, you simply find the difference between local noon and noon at the Greenwich meridian. Keeping in mind that the Earth makes a full circle around its axis in twenty-four hours, so one hour of time difference equals to 15 degrees of longitude."

"Is it the same for astronomy?" Director Pankins heard herself asking.

Miss Guide thought the director was being helpful by asking such a question, and answered her.

"Actually, you only need a sextant when you are on a ship. Considering the rocking waves, errors can occur. With a sextant and a chronometer, it eliminates those. On solid ground, you can do these calculations using a vertical rod, by measuring its height and the length of its shadow."

A pupil asked, "How can you do that at night?"

"Great question!" Miss Guide became excited to see her lesson interested the students.

"Anyone ever heard of the North Star?" Miss Guide asked.

This made Sirius think about her father, her mother, and her given last name. She began to think about her family and it made her sad to feel so unattached to anyone, kind of like a ship being tossed by waves, lost at sea.

Miss Guide said something as if she could read Sirius' thoughts, and it stunned her: "If you are ever lost at sea and need to get home, just look for the North Star."

CHAPTER 37

THE UNBEARABLE HURT

I woke the next day with my eyes so swollen I could barely see out of them.

"You can stay home, Holly Hocks, for today," my mom said as she pushed the hair back from my face, obviously seeing the swelling which had taken over. "I don't want you to fall behind in your schoolwork. Okay?"

She sat on my bed beside me, and said, "You do know you're only allowed to cry five hundred times in your life? And by my count, you have only twenty-five times left and you're only eight years old."

"Nine," I said.

"Yes, that's right. Falafel was a great dog and worthy of the tears you've shed for him. At some point you *will* feel better, I promise. Falafel wouldn't want you to be sad forever," my mom said. She gave me a kiss on my forehead and smoothed back my hair.

I nodded and crawled back in bed right after I grabbed Dookie. I put him under the covers and lifted them high above us, like we were in a tent. I watched him chug along, exploring the bed. He was so cute, and after some time I found myself smiling. I didn't think I could ever do that again.

Other than my moments with Dookie, life in general became bland and boring or really sad and lonely. All I could picture was poor Falafel's face right before he was killed. I cried myself to sleep knowing nothing could make me stop hurting for Falafel, and couldn't figure out how I, without Falafel, somehow managed to keep living.

My favorite holidays came and went without the joy I had once relished. I became almost empty until one day several months later, Begonia invited me to come to her house for a sleepover, which was the only thing that took my mind away from being sad. All week, I looked forward to going to her house. As soon as I arrived, we ran to go swimming in her *real* pool even though there was still a springtime freshness. I borrowed her goggles and floated around. Then I swam, pretending to be a mermaid. I swished my legs and kept them together to try to be as elegant as a "real" mermaid is, so effortlessly. In these moments I wished I had long hair. A short-haired mermaid in a mismatched bathing suit was not the image most people imagined when they thought of this mythical creature. So, as I pretended, Begonia reminded me of how un-mermaid-like I appeared.

"What are you doing?"

"I'm swimming like a mermaid."

"You look nothing like a mermaid—more like a sea cow."

Ouch.

She tried to demonstrate the grace and elegance one must have in order to be a *real* mermaid, and while her impersonation was probably much better than mine, it still fell way short.

We floated and splashed in the pool all day, until the sun started to set. Quickly the little warmth that graced the day was replaced with evening coolness. We jumped out of the pool as the shivers took over and ran into her house.

After we dressed, Begonia and I sat down to eat dinner; however, she decided she didn't like what was on the menu.

"I'm not eating this. It's gross!"

"Wha-da-ya mean, it's gross?" her mother asked.

Begonia pushed her plate of perfectly edible food away, while I waited to see how this would go down.

"Betula, make me pancakes," Begonia ordered. "Please," she added a tad late.

She did it again. She'd called her mother by her first name! And then, after a short, loud discussion, Begonia sat triumphantly eating her chocolate chip pancakes. Needless to say, I was not complaining because I shared in the spoils. I slurped the syrup, feeling full of guilt yet grateful for its yumminess. Mrs. Barley made the best pancakes, and she was the nicest mom out of all my friends' moms. She always wore a bandana in her hair as well as a genuine smile on her face.

After we ate, we watched television. Begonia's dad was home and this was my first time meeting him. He was out of town a lot for work. He was very different from my dad. He was Irish and he said words we weren't ever allowed to say in my home. I had difficulty understanding how to act around him, even though he was certainly outgoing and friendly. He and Begonia were having a fake wrestling match.

Of course I wanted in on the action, and when I lightly touched the bald spot at the top of his head, he said, "Touch it again, I tell ya, touch it again."

He sounded perturbed. I thought if I didn't touch his bald spot again, he'd for sure be angry with me. So I touched it again.

"Don't you evah touch that spot again! You hear me, you little turd?" (Except he had said the bad word.)

"I thought ...." I was utterly confused.

"Ned Barley!" Begonia's mother said sharply.

"Aww, I'm just yankin' her chain." He winked and asked, "How's your mom and dad?"

And his demeanor completely changed into super friendly Ned Barley. After I knew him better, I understood when he told me to touch his bald spot, he *did not* actually want me to touch his bald spot and that he was being facetious. That's when people tell you to do something and don't really want you to do it—at least, that's the definition I put together.

Begonia had a heavy genetic dosage of facetiousness. Actually, she was more of a brat, and mostly to her parents. They gave her whatever she wanted, and she pretended to be ungrateful. Or maybe she really wasn't pretending. I also noticed her room was a mess and her bed, which was large compared to mine, was never made. I really loved Begonia as a friend, so I decided since she had no brothers or sisters, it would be up to me to warn her about The Children's Horrible House.

"You might want to start being nicer to your mom and dad, and you should also start cleaning your room and making your bed," I informed her.

"Why? Are you gonna make me?"

She was keeping up her sassy act.

"I would if I were you," I said. "Otherwise you're going to be sent to The Children's Horrible House!"

"Huh?" she said.

"Where you work all day
and never, never play …
The Children's Horrible House … ahhh"

I sang the last part the way my brothers and sisters had sung it to me. She squinted at me, putting her hands on her hips. I tried another verse.

"You better clean your room
or you'll seal your doom … "

Begonia let out a laugh.

"I'm not kidding!"

"Yeah, okay, and I believe you …" She rolled her eyes.

I'm pretty sure she did not believe me.

"Why don't you ask Coriander, then?" I said.

Her face flashed to shock and then went to this state of bliss.

"Coriander?" she said his name as if it was her favorite.

"Yes, that's where I met him. He was there the same time I was."

"What is it? Where is it?" she asked.

"Um … I'm not sure where it is, but I can tell you what it's like."

"Tell me."

CHAPTER 38

THE CHILDREN'S HORRIBLE HOUSE

Staniel and Danley climbed high in the oak tree which seemed to lure children to its branches. From where they were perched, they could observe many different areas around the grounds of The Children's Horrible House. They sat silently, taking in the sounds and moments of stillness between the breezes, when at once both pairs of eyes focused on a man they had never seen before, walking toward the glowing garden. He appeared to be advanced in his age, yet conspicuously steady. They sat and watched him disappear into the circular maze surrounding the garden.

"You see that man?"

"Yup."

"Know who he is?"

"Nope."

"Think we should go check him out?"

"Yup."

The two identical boys climbed down like koalas and quietly made their way into the garden, careful to go undetected.

As they tiptoed through the maze and into the entry of the garden, at first they couldn't find the strange man and they became worried they may have lost him. They tucked themselves into the outer hedges, hoping to find the man as he walked. The peacocks casually strolled to and fro, having little interest in anything except bits of seeds dispersed on the ground. After a while, Staniel became restless and almost said something, when they saw the man exiting the tomb of Hawthorne North Star. He was holding something. Unfortunately, he had it clutched in his hand, hiding it from the twins' view.

CHAPTER 39

THE SPOOKY MAGICAL MANSION

"Okay …" I started saying, and then situated myself in a comfortable chair, as did Begonia. "It's this gigantic, creepy, old building or house, or,"—I cleared my throat and thought for a second how to properly describe the place—"um … okay. It's a house-ish, jail-ish, maroon-colored mansion."

Even though her face showed her confusion, I was kind of impressed with my descriptions so far and became more confident as I transformed into character and explained further.

"When I first arrived, the hairs on my arms stood up in fear from the building's spooky outdoor appearance." My voice became extra-eerie-sounding as I detailed the descriptions. "The unfortunate trees surrounding the house looked too frightened to be near it—they cowered in its shadow. It's on this enormous piece of carefully kept property with a huge stone wall that can only be accessed from the flaming gate entrance. Once inside, there's a hanging cage holding dangling kids who screamed out to me when I first arrived. *Buuut* … when I went inside the dark spooky mansion and explored it, the place was magical, and quite magnificent—it's the fanciest place I have ever seen! Still is! It had super-tall golden ceilings and stained-glass windows. The dining hall was beyond beautiful; it was spectacular … with a huge fireplace and pictures of old people all around. One was of Hawthorne North Star—he's the founder of The Hawthorne House for Children. The house used to be called that until his daughter, Saffron, also known as Director Sirius Pankins, changed the name to The Children's Horrible House, for reasons I do not know. Perhaps it's because there's a dark and dingy, smelly dungeon you were sent to if you talked back or even questioned something. So *you* would definitely be in THE DUNGEON a lot, especially if you talked to Director Pankins the way you talk to your parents."

Begonia gave me a skeptical look.

"It's true! I'm not lying," I protested.

Her look continued. I shouldn't have been surprised; I was just as unbelieving when my brothers and sisters tried to warn me. I told her about my time at The Children's Horrible House and she listened, but as I spoke, even *I* sensed it sounded exceedingly far-fetched.

"I met some other kids there too, Clover and twins named Staniel and Danley. We became really close friends and I think about them a lot. Sadly, I have no way to get in contact with them. I don't even know where they live."

"I knew some twins back home, but I can't remember their names."

"Where did you live before?" I asked.

"Buttonwood."

"Buttonwood? How far is that?"

"About five hours, I think, maybe?" She rubbed her chin, trying to gage the distance. "We make a lot of stops when we travel. I like to eat at all the cool restaurants along the way. My favorite stop is at RickyT's Pancake Piles. They have a griddle in the middle of the table where you can make your own pancakes. I make mine with chocolate chips, bananas, and whipped cream."

"Of course you do." I giggled.

Begonia ate fancier food than what I was used to. She and her parents went to restaurants where you ordered food from this thing called a menu. If we went out, it was only on Sundays after church, at either a Chinese buffet, or Moosewood's Cafeteria where we ate our food from an assembly line of overflowing food troughs.

"The Children's Horrible House, huh?" she pondered.

"Yup." I nodded a tad too hard and caused a cramp in my neck. "Ouch." I tried to rub it away … with little relief.

"Doesn't sound too scary."

"It's not … but it is. … Does that make any sense?"

"No, but who cares? It's not like the place is real, anyway."

I remembered when I used to think the same thing.

CHAPTER 40

WHAT'S GOING ON?

The next day at school I made a beeline for Coriander, who was already talking with Begonia. He quickly turned, looked at me briefly, and walked away.

"What's going on?" I asked Begonia.

"I asked him about The Children's Horrible House and he wouldn't say a thing. Are you playing a trick on me?" She looked at me in her skeptical manner.

"No, I don't know why he might be upset. It's not like it was supposed to be a secret."

"Apparently, he doesn't want me to know about it, then."

Begonia seemed confused. She was used to getting anything she wanted. And she wanted to get Coriander to like her.

"I'll get to the bottom of this," I promised as I left to go catch Coriander.

When I caught up to him, he was about to enter the classroom. I tugged his shirt and said, "Wait."

"I have class."

"I know. Just give me a second."

"Okay, time's up."

"Are you mad at me?"

"A little."

"Why?"

"You shouldn't have told anyone."

"Why?"

He shifted his eyes, looking for an answer. "Um … it's … okay but you haven't talked to me in weeks and then this? I don't know why, but do you want the whole world knowing about the treasure when we are so close to figuring it out for ourselves?"

"Are we close?"

He started to say something right when the bell rang for classes to begin.

"I'll talk to you later," he said as he went into his class.

CHAPTER 41

THE CHILDREN'S HORRIBLE HOUSE HEADED HOME

With all the confusion of Reed Trustworthy's return from the dead and all the new astronomical information she'd taken in recently, Sirius felt like she was sweeping leaves on a windy day—making menial strokes of frustrating progress. So there was some hope, though the treasure still stayed out of her reach. Even as she tossed and turned in her sleep, strange images kept appearing in her dreams, which made it so even sleeping kept her restless.

In her dream, Sirius was on a giant ship with huge masts, being assaulted by ultra-heavy rain and wind. She was within a chamber, rocking to and fro from the savage forces. Abruptly she felt sick. She ran out of her room and up the stairs to the main deck. When she came to the port side rail, the storm had passed and all the sails hung, ripped to shreds, causing the boat to drift aimlessly. She peered over the side, into the water, and saw sharks circling and jostling one another. How would she get home? She searched for the crew and found them passed out from all the ruckus. A light swayed near the ship's steering wheel. She saw a man who must be the captain of the ship, and tottered over hoping to find out where they were headed and when they might arrive. As she slowly walked toward him, holding on to various steady objects, she discovered where he was looking. Right in front of her in the cloudless speckled sky, shined the North Star, hanging brightly at the tail of Ursa Minor.

The captain's hat was regal, large, and shadowed his face. As Saffron came closer, something felt familiar about the man's posture. In an instant, the captain now sat at a desk, recording his calculations within his private quarters of the ship—no longer at the ship's wheel. The captain's quarters resembled the H.N. Star library's upper observatory, filled with volumes of books, charts, various astronomical instruments, and a large range of scopes.

Without her even asking, the captain said, "Saffron, we're headed home."

It was her father's voice speaking, the moment before she opened her eyes.

Covered in sweat, she gasped for breath. She raised herself and threw off the covers. Sirius sat there for some time and gathered herself together. Her uneven breath slowly started to steady. With the images from her dream fresh in her head, she replayed them, as well as the sound of her father's voice as if it had been recorded. *Saffron, we're headed home.* … Headed home? she wondered. How could they head home when they weren't even alive? It must have been a dream. She couldn't help imagining what it might be like if her parents did come home. How would living together as a family once again be?

Would it be awkward or uncomfortable? She preferred to imagine it as wonderful, and lay back, thinking of her fantasy life with her parents as she drifted back to sleep.

CHAPTER 42
PULLING FINGERS

I couldn't wait for PE, when I'd be able to talk to Coriander. The day seemed to be lengthening from minutes to hours in tremendous, sluggish time periods. I even fell asleep at one point and was woken by my body jerking involuntarily. Apparently I hadn't been sleeping for too long because the only one who noticed was a greasy-haired boy who looked around and then at me and extended his pointed index finger.

"Pull it," he whispered.

I knew the old *pull my finger trick*, but I was too sleepy to laugh at the fart he let out even though no one pulled the trigger. It sounded like a balloon leaking trapped air: *PFFFFFFFFEEERRRRIT!*

"Gross!" I held my nose, waiting for the overpowering stink to pass.

I was fully awake after class and I had more energy. I skipped along to PE, looking at my less-new pink sneakers. The Velcro wasn't staying as gripped as before, but the shoes were still cool and fast. I saw Coriander kicking around the ball and asked him if we could spar. We took turns passing the ball to one another, and Coriander showed off his skills juggling and bouncing the balls off his knees to the side of his foot and then his head. My best move was getting the ball from the other person; other than that, my game wasn't so spectacular.

Inside my head, I imagined myself as a great athlete. In real life, I tried to make up for my lack of coordination by being extra-enthusiastic. I wasn't a total goof. However, no one had ever encouraged me to pursue any sports as a career.

After our practice, I couldn't pretend like everything was normal, so I asked Coriander, "Are you ever going to talk to me?"

"About what?"

"Don't play dumb. How come you're so upset about me telling Begonia? You know she really should go. She's kind of spoiled and her room is a mess."

Coriander's expression changed into something like excitement. He plunged a fist into a front pants pocket and pulled it out quickly.

"See this? I'm going back." He opened his palm, exposing a large crystal.

I was taken off guard by his bold statement and the object in his hand. "Whe-where did you get that?"

"From the attic at The Children's Horrible House."

"You can do that? You can go back anytime?" I asked while reaching out to hold it.

But he was putting it back in his pocket. "I did it before. I'll do it again. Want to go with me?"

I thought about it. Without Falafel, life in general passed with little joy. The only time, I became excited was when I talked about The Children's Horrible House to Begonia. I remembered how scared I was when I first arrived and how intimidating Director Pankins could be and how I felt double-crossed by Miss Judge. I also felt cheated; I had unfinished business there, as did Coriander.

"I do."

CHAPTER 43

Stuck at
THE CHILDREN'S HORRIBLE HOUSE

"When can I go home?" Juniper asked Major Whoopins as he was passing her in the hallway.

"Up t' Miss Pankins." His eyes grew big, punctuating his serious statement.

"I've been here a long time, and I haven't found my sister, Holly, and I'm getting worried. Can you please ask her for me?"

"I see what I can do … cain't promise nuthin', though."

"Thank you, Major Whoopins." Juniper turned and scuffed away.

Major Whoopins could sense her fears and took pity on the poor girl. He went and knocked on the director's door.

"Who's there?"

"Me, the Major Whoopins."

"Come in."

"Good mornin', ma'am. … Um, that girl, Juniper, the sister of that Holly girl?"

"Yes, go on."

"She ready to go home and she scared fo' her sister."

"And?"

"What do I tell her?"

"Tell her this," Director Pankins said as she wrote a note and handed it to him.

CHAPTER 44
THE LETTER

Something very strange happened today. Hyperion, Juniper's boyfriend, showed up at our house holding Filbert. Consequently, I was not excited about the dumb missing dog. All I wanted to know was where my Juniper had been.

No one else except Ginger was home and she was busy being beautiful. I answered the door, eager for information on Juniper.

A young man stood at the door in stone-washed jeans and a jean jacket with the collar flipped up. I kind of knew who he was. I wanted to be sure before I said something stupid.

"Hello, may I help you?"

"Hi! Holly, is it?" He smiled nervously. "My name is Hyperion and—"

"Where's Juniper?" I asked, stopping him before he could tell me anything more.

"Isn't she home?" Hyperion said, handing me the dumb dog.

"I thought she was with you," I said, after setting Filbert on the floor and petting him for a bit before he ran off—of course.

"No, she stopped talking to me a while ago. She asked me to

give her a ride; she said she was looking for you at your grandparents' home. She had me drop her off at this gigantic, creepy mansion. I told her it didn't look safe. But she insisted I let her go."

"You let her go?"

"It wasn't my idea. … We argued before she got out of my car, and I haven't heard from her since. I assumed she was okay, being at your grandparents' house, but I couldn't stand it any longer. I came here to talk to her. Oh, by the way, here's your mail. I guess the mailman was too lazy to bring it all the way over here himself."

Hyperion handed me a small stack of letters and set down a small box. I flipped through the bills and other non-important pieces of mail and was about to put them aside when one small piece fell to the floor. I bent down and picked up a paper folded into an intricate origami-shaped note—not the usual letter. The note was addressed to me and had a pull-down tab for me to open. It was a little too familiar. As soon as I unfurled the note, I read:

Dear Holly,
Will you
Plase come happle me
mock my beds.
♥, Juniper
P.S. They won't let me leave until you come back.

My eyes practically popped. This note was the real deal.

"Where did you get this?" I asked.

Hyperion peered behind him as if he might be in trouble or something. "Like I said, the mailman handed these to me as I was coming in." He hesitated briefly, and then asked, "What's going on?", as he scratched his head.

"I'm not sure. You say you dropped her off at some big, creepy house? Did it have a big iron gate that appeared to be on fire?"

"Please tell me that was your grandparents' house!"

"Not exactly, but I know where I need to go."

"Where?"

"It's a secret. Thanks, Hyperion. I will tell her to call you when she gets back."

That seemed to make him happy and he smiled as I closed the door.

Ginger came in, holding Filbert proudly.

"You did it! You found Filbert like you promised, Holly!" Ginger's approval was all I had ever really wanted, besides all the other things a kid like me wants, and it felt so great to think she now might like me … but I couldn't mislead her.

"I didn't actually find Filbert," I confessed. "Hyperion, Juniper's boyfriend, did, and he brought him back."

"I should have known a wart-topped skin tag like you wouldn't be able to find him, or your own shadow, for that matter."

Ouch.

"Just kidding, Butt Wipe." She tickled the top of my head, gave me a wink, and said casually, "Maybe the big guy upstairs answered someone's prayers."

"Huh?" I asked, shocked to think that what she said might be possible.

"I knew you'd come back! I knew it," she said while nuzzling the dumb dog's neck. Filbert loved her attention and it made me happy to see them so.

CHAPTER 45

THE CHILDREN'S HORRIBLE HOUSE

"Think we heddin' back to git them kids," Major Whoopins informed Mr. Ree.

"Man, what are you talking about?"

"Miss Pankins say she want 'em back."

"Which ones?"

"The bunny-hat-wearing girl and the quiet, sneakin', snoopin' boy."

Mr. Ree scanned his brain trying to pick out which kids Major Whoopins was talking about. Most kids came to The Children's Horrible House once … once. However, those two particular kids were far less forgettable than the others.

"She said that?"

"That's a fact."

"Are you talking about Holly Spinatsch and Coriander Oats?"

"Yeauh."

"She wants 'em back again?"

"Yeauh."

Mr. Ree breathed out in exhaustion. "Man, I'm tired. We are just back from bringing in a new load of kids."

Without waiting for any more complaints, Major Whoopins said, "We can hit up RickyT's on the way."

"Now we're talkin'. I've had a hankering for some hotcakes with blueberries, strawberries, and maple syrup."

"Think I'm goin' git some hash brown, sausage, biscuits too!" Major Whoopins licked his lips, anticipating his soon-to-be meal.

"Don't forget the orange marmalade and hot tea," Mr. Ree threw in.

Major Whoopins gave him a look of *You got to be kiddin' me.*

CHAPTER 46

AIR BRAKES

I called Coriander to tell him about the note, but he wasn't home. I called over and over. My fingers began to ache at the sheer amount of times I dialed his number.

"I'm sorry, Holly. I'll let him know to call you right back as soon as he comes home," Mrs. Oats said apologetically.

"Do you know where he went?" I asked.

"No, dear, he was gone before I came home from work. I'm sure he'll be home for supper."

"Okay, Mrs. Oats, thank you." I hung up the phone.

I paced my house, wanting to get back to The Children's Horrible House as quickly as possible. I was weirdly excited. This time I knew what to expect. I had already gone through the whole process where you meet Miss Take and her fingers dance all over the keyboard like a ballerina on Broadway, where Miss Diagnosis checks vision, hearing, spine, and hair for lice with her three-inch-thick, twenty-pound glasses trying to rip her nose from her face, and where Miss Shapen slops disgusting meals onto trays with her sloshing, overfilled, water balloon body.

I called Begonia too, and told her what happened. I also told her more details about The Children's Horrible House I had forgotten to tell her before.

"You think your sister's there?" she asked.

"She has to be. She wrote the note the same way I had written to her, to let me know it's her. Only she would know that."

Actually, after Juniper and Cashew read it over and over again, my whole family knew about the letter I had written to Juniper, asking for her assistance to help me make my bed. Since I was a terrible speller, it became a joke and I was the butt of it. Now it had been used as a secret code and it kind of made me proud and excited.

I told Begonia to come over as soon as possible. I could hardly contain myself. I went upstairs and changed into my most comfortable outfit—you guessed it, my Oscar the Grouch T-shirt and cutoff corduroys. My hat almost never left my head, so that was accounted for, and I packed some of my things until dark. I felt anxious, like I couldn't wait to get this show on the road. I had to find a way to calm myself. Dookie was exercising, making rounds on his wheel when I grabbed him. I needed his comfort. I sat back on my bed, letting him crawl around on my chest and onto my face.

"Dookie, you're so cute. I bet you are the cutest hamster in the whole wide world."

His dark beady eyes barely blinked, but I could tell he enjoyed my attention. He crawled around, and I turned over, making my arms into various bridges he could cross under. I started imagining my bed was made out of water and I was a giant sea monster in a huge ocean, sneaking up on unsuspecting boats while Dookie bravely saved them.

Abruptly, I heard air brakes whistle and a door open. I rubbed my eyes, unaware I had drifted off. Drool still hung from the side of my mouth and I sipped it back in. I heard feet shuffling and jumped out of bed. I looked out of my window and saw the white bus. I ran downstairs, almost forgetting my sneakers. I slid them on without securing them, all while closely holding Dookie.

I opened the front door and saw Major Whoopins and Mr. Ree standing as official as ever, pretending to not be pleased to see me. Secretly, I could see a sparkle in their eyes and a slight smile on their lips.

The white bus, with its haunting letters spilled down the sides, dared me to board it. The sinister bus was like a scary ice cream truck that played horrific organ music while promising disgusting food. I wanted to get in, but was reluctant now that it stood in front of me. I think boarding this bus would always be frightening and fascinating.

Mr. Ree had syrup dripping from his chin and I thought about telling him. Major Whoopins gestured for me to board the bus, when I realized I was forgetting something.

"Oh, no! I forgot about—"

"No time for wastin'. You git up in there so's we can be on our way." Major Whoopins gave me a small pat.

"But …"

"Holly, come on, let's go!"

That was Coriander's voice from inside the bus. I peeked in and climbed the steps. Immediately they closed the door and I barely had time to sit and get comfortable.

"I forgot …" I exhaled in frustration.

Then I heard, "Boo!" from behind me.

It wasn't Coriander's voice. I turned and saw Begonia, giggling in glee and holding her hands above her head like she was a moose.

Coriander tried to look serious. Reluctantly, he smiled as he stared out the window.

"Begonia! How did you get here?"

"Why don't you ask Coriander?"

I looked back at him and he shrugged; his look told me everything.

Begonia's excitement was barely containable. She managed to get herself under control. When the music came on, her eyes grew scared with the deep-and-low haunting tones coming from the speakers. The excitement she was once filled with was replaced with captivation.

"The Children's Horrible House
The Children's Horrible House
Where you work all day and never, never play
The Children's Horrible House … ahhh!"

"It's okay, Begonia," I said. "We're all in this together … you, me, Coriander, and Dookie … *Dookie*?" Dookie was patiently wiggling his nose while I held him in my sweaty hands. I realized that I forgot to put Dookie away in his cage. I knew I was forgetting something! "Oh, no! What am I going to do now?" I flung my head back in despair.

Begonia came to my seat and gently took Dookie out of my grasp. "Come here, Dookie. Aren't you the cutest little morsel of milk chocolate!" She nuzzled him and said, "We will all look after Dookie. We'll keep him safe with us."

I should have known she'd try to give me some measure of assurance to put me at ease.

"What will he eat?" Coriander asked, and the ease I almost felt disappeared.

I wondered the same thing. Then I recalled the wilted lettuce, brown apples, and cold cheese chunks served regularly in the dining hall at The Children's Horrible House.

"I don't think that will be the problem, remember?"

Coriander thought and said, "What about if he gets loose and we can't find him?"

"Dookie's a good hamster. He never runs away, and …" I quickly became fearful. However, I resolutely decided to guard my Dookie with my life.

"We *all* will take care of Dookie," Begonia stated with finality, and I thought about the time Begonia took care of me when Kale Collard punched me. She'd look after Dookie because that's what Begonia did for people *and* pets, and I couldn't ask for a better friend or any more reassurance.

The bus traveled along the road, and I realized I didn't think enough to turn around and see my house disappear. I was too excited and anxious about the trip. I wondered how long the ride would last, as most kids do, and recalled the last time I had taken this trip, it seemed to pass quickly. I looked over at Begonia, who played with Dookie. She was a natural when it came to taking care of animals. At the same time I worried about Dookie, he seemed to make her feel better.

My mind was racing in all directions. When I became quiet in my thoughts, I sensed a static in the air … until I tuned in to Coriander and the deep thoughts echoing from his head. He had one thing on his brain—treasure. My thoughts rolled around like bubbles that popped when my mind went to a new contemplation. I couldn't wait to see Juniper and wondered how she was doing at The Children's Horrible House. Was she making any friends? I wondered if she had to go to **THE DUNGEON**. Juniper was pretty obedient, so I doubted if she ever was silly enough to get caught doing something that deserved such punishment. I wondered if Clover and the PP twins were still there or if they, too, were sent home. The anticipation was exciting and annoying at once.

The trees passed by like we were going through a time warp—especially with the rainbow-tinted glass on the bus windows. My eyes darted back and forth, trying to keep up with them, as the forest disappeared behind us. My mind became foggy and the colors all blurred into a spiraling hypnotic trance as the spooky music softly played.

The bus' air brakes let out a *squeak* as it agilely stopped. I opened my eyes, expecting to see the huge flaming gate welcoming us back to The Children's Horrible House. That is not what I saw. I also did not see the bowing trees offering us a formal welcome. The bus doors opened and Major Whoopins called out, telling us to get off.

"Where are we?" I asked.

Begonia's face seemed confused, like I was supposed to know where we were. Dookie looked at me too. I turned back to Coriander, who stood trying to become aware of our location. All he did was shrug.

"Let's go," Major Whoopins commanded.

We jumped up and gathered our belongings and exited the bus. Before us stood a large two-story stable house. It looked familiar in its details and structure, but I was certain I had never seen this place before. We were in the middle of nowhere and the trees which bordered the property cowered in fear.

Major Whoopins unlatched the gigantic double door and led us inside to what had to be the spookiest stable house ever. This must be where the headless horseman kept his demon horse. I could see more of the interior chambers as Major Whoopins gradually lit more gas lanterns. Cobwebs dripped from the center hall that ran along a number of empty stalls. Old hay carpeted the floor and more was stacked along the far walls. A loft above us had a wooden ladder leading up to it.

"Excuse me, Major Whoopins, where are we?" I asked, hoping our previous mutual kinship might help in answering my question.

"You find out soon as it time. In tha meantime, mi' as well make yo'selves at home. You gon' be here a while."

"What about food? I'm starving," Begonia moaned.

"Someone be along soon with somethin' for y'all to eat," he promised.

After they left us a pile of blankets and pillows to sleep on, Major Whoopins and Mr. Ree shut the door behind them.

"How are we going to sleep out here? It smells, and I'm starving," Begonia whined.

With a certain expression, Coriander silently told me to get my friend under control.

I said, "Begonia, I'm sorry. This is not what I expected, at all. I shouldn't have talked you into coming here."

She exhaled in despair, but continued to watch over Dookie. Dookie calmed her more than anything else.

Coriander shook the doors, testing them for escape; they were locked solid. He stalked through the rest of the stables, seeing if there was any other way out, while I stood wondering if I should look with him or stay to comfort Begonia. What I actually accomplished was a whole lot of nothing.

Boredom set in, as well as grumbling bellies from all three of us. I arranged the blankets and pillows as decoratively as possible, hoping any dash of comfort might lighten the gloom that enveloped this place.

Out of the silence, footsteps could be heard crunching in the gravel … coming closer and closer, outside the door.

Begonia stuck her fingers in her mouth as if she wanted to bite her nails. Coriander stood like a soldier. I closed my eyes, hoping this nightmare would come to an end … when the door creaked open. I was afraid to open my eyes, as the person who opened the door ran inside, and bowled me over like a pin. My body crashed back to the floor as I slowly understood that someone with a particularly familiar voice was speaking and exclaiming excitement.

I opened my eyes and saw Juniper! I realized she had actually been hugging me and telling me how glad she was to see me.

"Holly Hocks! You got my note! I knew you'd understand. I had to be careful due to … well, you know." Juniper stopped and looked around. "They're always watching." Her blue eyes grew and then softened as she rejoiced in our reunion. "I'm so glad you're here!"

"Juniper, why did you come here?"

"I was looking for you, silly."

"Didn't you know where I was?"

"Yes, but I became worried. … Pluth, I mithed you," she said, making her voice turn into the little baby voice she used when being sentimental.

"I mithed you too," I said, and we hugged again.

I giggled when she made a silly mouse-like expression.

"When do you think we are going to eat?" Begonia asked. She looked as if she was on the verge of panic or dying if she didn't eat soon.

"Oh! I brought you guys some food. It's in a basket outside the door. I had to set it down in order to open that heavy thing." Juniper jumped up and we all followed her to the door, ready to mow down anything remotely edible. I should have guessed. Go ahead … give it a try …. Yup, wilted lettuce cheese wraps and brown apples. For a much appreciated bonus, there was a brownie—at least that's what it resembled. When I bit into it, it bit me back, almost chipping my tooth. The hockey puck brownie-thing was so hard it was inedible.

Phooey.

I easily managed to save some scraps for Dookie, as did Begonia, who fed him at the same time she ate.

Having Juniper with me made all the difference in the world. She was my comfort and my entertainment. In fact, she entertained us all with her array of impersonations.

"So there I was in the awwfice of Directa Pankins. … She thaawwt she could intimidate me, she did, so I says, I'm heah faw my sistah, Hawlly Spinach. An I ain't leavin' witout harh!"

Begonia and I giggled as Juniper relentlessly told us her tales in her finest northern accent. At first, Coriander didn't want to participate in the show, preferring to scope out our situation. He walked around, calculating his next move. He had put a stick in the door to make sure we wouldn't be locked inside again. As soon as he felt somewhat satisfied with understanding our predicament, he sat with us in the circle while Juniper relived her experiences at The Children's Horrible House.

"So, where exactly are we?" Coriander asked out of the blue.

In the distance the unmistakable cry of the white peacocks that lived in the glowing garden could be heard. All of our eyes bulged and then we shivered, knowing exactly where we were.

CHAPTER 47

THE CHILDREN'S HORRIBLE HOUSE

"They here, Miss Pankins," Major Whoopins informed her.

"Good. Make sure to keep them away from the general population. They are to be kept secluded so I can keep a better eye on them. … I have an idea of what they'll be doing," she said as if this was all part of her devious plans.

"Yes, ma'am. Mr. Meanor is on the watch." Major Whoopins nodded. "I sent the sista to bring 'em sumthin' ta eat. They got a friend too, name's …." Major Whoopins whipped his clipboard from behind his back and searched for the information regarding the new girl's identity. "Okay, let's see here … um … okay, here it is. Begonia Barley."

Miss Pankins' eyes constricted as she took in the information, but what caught her eye was rising outside of her window. She saw clouds swimming around the moon, holding it under their cover and then mercifully letting it out for air. The sullen moon appeared frightened to be seen and Sirius looked directly into it and said, "I see you." She thought she only spoke the words telepathically. When Major Whoopins sounded uncomfortable with his " 'Scuze me, ma'am?", she waved him off as if she meant to tell him that, as well.

"That will be all."

CHAPTER 48

THE CRYSTAL CAVE

None of us could get comfortable. The hay poked us and scratched us to no end. The only one who seemed content in all this mess was Dookie. This barn or stable was like his personal playground. Dookie scurried around from corner to corner, doing strange tricks I didn't even know he could do. Begonia found a ball-shaped nut that he pushed around like he was a soccer player. He didn't do the rolling aimlessly; he rolled it around within the circle of our makeshift campout. Dookie kept us entertained until we heard the peacocks once again cry out.

Coriander stood and said, "I'm going to the glowing garden. Anyone care to join me?" He glowered specifically at me, but everyone was ready to get out of this place, too.

I dusted off the hay and put on my sneakers. Coriander moved the stick he had placed inside the door to keep us from being trapped, and we all spilled out from the barn, onto the crunchy gravel.

"You worms don't think you're going anywhere, do you?" a voice boomed out from the darkness.

Juniper protectively wrapped her arms around me and Begonia squeezed her way inside our embrace.

"Who's there?" Coriander asked.

"Get back inside, if you know what's good for you stinkin' brats."

We scrambled back into the stable. Coriander didn't move as quickly as the voice preferred.

"Now!"

The door slammed behind us. We stood inside the stable, once again trapped.

"Why would they bring us all the way here … to keep us hostage … in this poop-smelling, rotten old barn?" Coriander said between huffs.

We were all perplexed. Why couldn't we stay in The Children's Horrible House? The once tolerable mood vanished. Coriander did not like being trapped; he skirted around the gigantic stable looking for an escape. As he frantically searched, we girls gave in to our exhaustion. We piled onto each other's softest spots, seeking any kind of rest.

My consciousness kept going in and out like a television antenna searching for a station. I'd fall asleep so quickly and then as swiftly be woken dozens of times, until Coriander shook me awake.

"I found a way out of here. Come on, let's go."

Without hesitation I stood and followed him to a back corner of the stable, not realizing I was still half asleep. He lifted a hatch and, with his oil lamp, showed me a deep, dark tunnel.

"Come on." He swished his hair in the direction of the tunnel.

I groggily asked, "What about the others?"

"I'm not sure if this will get us anywhere and if we get caught, I don't want us all to get in trouble."

I reluctantly peeked inside the creepy, dark tunnel and imagined monsters waiting to attack me. I hesitated.

Coriander said impatiently, "Let's go!"

"Okay, okay. … Give me a sec." I breathed in and gathered the necessary courage to take the first step.

"Why do I have to go first?" I asked.

"*Move.*" He pushed past me, looked back, held out his hand, and said, "Come on."

"Um … I'm scared."

"Want me to hold your hand?" he asked in a mocking mommy-baby manner that lit an angry fire and spurred me to cast my fears aside.

"No!" I blurted out.

"Then, c'mon," he said as he turned to walk into the tunnel, whether I followed him or not.

"Wait! I'm coming …" I quickly caught up to him and even though I refused to hold his hand, I found myself holding onto his arm in a death grip.

"Take it easy. You're going to cut off my circulation."

"Oh, sorry." I eased up on my hold.

The tunnel opened wider the farther we went inside. The walls must have been made from the same material as the walls of THE DUNGEON, the torturous chamber at the bottom pit of The Children's Horrible House. Just thinking about the smells that seeped from that damp, dark cell gave me chills. I shook them off, and Coriander gave me a look with one of his eyebrows lifted while the other brow stayed down, telling me that I was weird.

Up ahead, the dark tunnel showed some light coming from a wider section of its never-ending vein. Was someone else within it? We quietly traversed farther and farther, until the glow became more and more brilliant. Sparkling rocks began to dot the walls. They became even more plentiful the closer we came to the mysterious illuminated section. Before I knew it, we were surrounded by brilliant, glowing, clear-spiked rocks projecting out from the ground and growing downward from the ceiling. The tunnel became a cavern filled with crystals which seemed to glow all on their own. We stood speechless.

Coriander and I gazed in awe at this amazing space which was out of this world. I could feel an energy coming from the stones, and its signal was strong. It felt like a vibrating, penetrating force that could transport you to another dimension. It reminded me of Superman's house, when he chose to become mortal for Lois Lane—what a mistake that was. This place was even more brilliant, with an array of colors ranging from ice blue, turquoise, and even purple. The kaleidoscopic cave was unbelievable; I almost couldn't believe it myself.

"This is the coolest place I have ever seen," I said, breaking the silence, and my voice echoed millions of times off each crystal, sending an echo back and forth through the tunnel.

Coriander silently shushed me. I put my hand over my mouth when I heard the loudness I had accidentally reverberated.

We walked all around and it seemed like the cave could possibly continue on infinitely, though in the distance it was too tight for us to explore further. There was a shaft in the center of the cave that reached from the floor to the ceiling. I stepped over to it and turned when I could feel someone behind me. I froze, scared to move, when I idiotically realized a floor-length mirror exhibited my own boorish reflection. I wondered what a mirror was doing inside this crystal cave. The mirror wasn't hanging. Actually, it blossomed out, yet was encrusted into the wall—surrounded by smaller crystals. As I stared into the mirror, an image stared back. It looked like me, but notably different. My scaredy-cat senses kept spooking me and then … it blinked when I did not.

Chills ran through my spine and I shook. Then the image realigned with my own, leaving a shape that at first was not visible. As I stared, it became clearly outlined within the glass—the circular cross, the same cross found throughout the grounds here at The Children's Horrible House. I stared at the symbol within my reflection, and everything spun from left to right in a hypnotic, trance-inducing twist. I felt like I was being sucked into the mirror. My breath quickened and I felt something tugging at my abdomen. I heard a squealing scream which should have broken the mirror, echoing from within as it pulled me harder. I felt my body almost give in and let it have me … and it almost did, when out of nowhere, it stopped.

Maybe my vision and senses were being tricked, so I quickly blinked. When my eyes reopened, the shape and my image stood still but my knees felt wobbly.

There was a deep yet subtle vibration still echoing from the wall. I touched the edges to steady myself.

"OUCH!" It felt nuclear hot and I pulled my hand away quickly, thinking it had been burned. I stood back, not wanting to provoke the mirror any more. I held my hand and cradled it, but found no sign of a wound. It felt magically fine.

I turned to see Coriander, who was looking closer at a crystal with a deeper, more purple color. He hadn't even been aware that I was almost sucked inside the monstrous mirror. He continued to examine his crystal without a care in the world for my safety. The crystal projected from a base like a nature-made control panel. He touched it ever so slightly, when a screeching sound similar to what I had heard seconds prior, blared throughout the cave. A rumbling followed; it seemed as if the whole tunnel might collapse around us.

We ran back as fast as we could, tripping and falling, trying to escape, scrambling for our lives. When we found the hatch, it wouldn't open. The rumbling came closer and closer. Coriander pushed with all of his might and then I pushed too, and the hatch finally gave way. We came up and out panting, feeling on the verge of certain death. Oh, that's right, we *were* on the verge of certain death.

We staggered back to check on Begonia, Dookie, and Juniper. In the place that once held their sleeping bodies, lay only a couple of pieces of hay that formed an arrow pointing to the ladder that led to the loft.

We climbed the ladder all the way to the top, hoping to see them. Still no sight of Juniper, Begonia … or Dookie. Coriander searched the space until he found a window that opened out like the hatch that led to the tunnel. Only, this hatch opened to a line of wire that could take someone away from the stable in a hurry.

"It's a zip line," Coriander said.

"Where are the handles?" I asked.

"Good question. I'm going to bet they are out there with them." Coriander pointed into the distance.

He quickly turned and scurried back to the ladder and climbed down. I followed him and poked my head over the loft to see what he was doing. He ran for some rags and a tool, grabbed them, and climbed back up the ladder.

"What's that?"

"I don't know what it's called, but if you hold tight to me, it will get us to the end of the line."

He wrapped my hands around his waist, securing them with the rags, and then his hands around the handles. He instructed me to hold tight … and we zipped and dipped across the line.

"Yippee!" I squealed as we quickly descended to the ground.

The line ended hundreds of yards away from the stable.

Plop! We landed a little ungracefully in a pile and Coriander was sitting on my head.

"Get off my face, I'm suffocating!" my muffled voice croaked.

He squirmed around and fumbled to his feet, and then extended his hand to help me while we still struggled, tangled together in the rags.

After we undid the tethers, we continued our search for Juniper and Begonia—and Dookie. The air felt dead, still, and damp. I wished I had packed a sweatshirt or something; the T-shirt and cords were not keeping me warm. I wasn't sure if my nerves made me shiver or if the weather seemed strange. Thankfully, my bunny hat kept my head from being exposed to the nighttime elements. I wrapped the ears around my chin and was a tad more comforted.

Coriander looked around and signaled for me to follow. There was a foot trail in the grounds, leading to something tremendous which induced my body to shudder. The branches from the last trees we passed whipped back behind us as we came upon the dark-shadowed silhouette of the formidable building that was none other than The Children's Horrible House.

It stood daring us to intrude on its gargantuan stateliness. It seemed angry with us, watching even our slightest move. We stood there intimidated, yet in awe of the amazing presence this house held.

Coriander whispered, "Well, we're back."

"Yes, we are," I agreed quietly.

Even our whispers echoed into each other, as if voices other than ours quietly muttered. This place held more secrets than could ever be discovered. Even the secrets had secrets and they were secretly keeping them to themselves.

CHAPTER 49

THE HUGGING TREE

The trail continued, going in another direction. As we came to the end of it, the circular maze surrounding the glowing garden on the far side of the property came into view.

"I know exactly where we are now!" I exclaimed.

"Duh," Coriander playfully said when we practically galloped to the maze entrance.

Before me was the place where dreams formed and lasted forever. I couldn't wait to go inside. I put my hands on the circular cross symbol and pushed open the squeaking iron gate. We jogged through the mazes and of course we became lost. No one could not get lost once or twice in the maze; the trail became new every time.

I was glad Coriander was with me, considering he seemed to have a natural compass in his head. In the maze, even Coriander's natural instincts were questioned.

After too many setbacks, we almost quit … until we, by chance, came to the real grand entrance and stepped under the arch, into the opening of the most majestic place on the planet. This was close to what the Tinsel Tree Forest looked like in my imagination. Unbelievably, here was better than my fantasy life. My mom often said fantasies were better than realities. In this case, the reality was above and beyond my expectations.

I took in the glowing orbs floating around like dreams waiting to be visualized. The weeping willow seemed to be crying tears of joy, heavy in its foliage. I waved hello and could swear it swayed back, recognizing me. I glided over to it and lifted the gentle string of leaves, and smiled. I dipped under the enormous sheet of bowing branches and came within the tree's embrace and hugged it back.

"You a tree hugger?" Coriander joked.

"Yup, you wanna give it a hug too?"

Coriander at first acted like hugging a tree was foolish. Then the tree must have spoken to him as well. He bent under the drooping branches and the three of us hugged one another. The hug was exactly what we needed to continue our quest.

Luminescent flowers and plants illuminated in sequence as we stepped and I felt like I was living a dream. The orbs floated around us like satellites circling the Earth. Buzzing from the fireflies and phosphorescent dragonflies softly sang in my ears while moonflowers started to unfurl.

One flower, in particular, I had to see and smell. I stepped through the ground coverings until I came face-to-face with the arbor holding the beautiful purple-faced passionflower. I stuck my whole face within the giant blooms and let the little yellow spines tickle my nose.

"Achoo!" I tried to muffle my sneeze, but it made the next one stronger. "Achoo!" "Achoo!" … Seven sneezes in all, and I could have slapped my own face. What did I do! All the tiptoeing and whispering, trying to be stealthy, blew up like a noise bomb with my untimely reaction. Hopefully, no one had heard me.

"Bless you," I heard a short distance away. *Great*, obviously someone heard me. Who was it? It seemed to have come from the mausoleum.

Was it a ghost? Oh, no! I wasn't ready to see a ghost! Most ghosts aren't so polite. I reconsidered. If it wasn't a ghost, it was probably a person whom I may not want to see, yet. Bushes started moving, and I almost wet my pants … until Begonia and Juniper popped their heads out from the other side of the plant.

"You guys, you scared me!"

They giggled and shoved me around in jest.

"Where's Coriander?" Begonia asked.

I glanced behind me, thinking we had been together this whole time, but he was not visible. In the distance, I heard the faint sound of rumbling thunder.

I shrugged my shoulders and saw Dookie poking out from Begonia's shirt pocket.

"Hey there, little guy." I melted when I saw his tiny face, and went to grab him and give him the love he so deserved. Somehow he fell from my hands and disappeared into the thick ground cover.

"Oh, no! Dookie!" I was afraid to move for fear I might accidentally crush him. "Guys! Oh, my gosh. Help me find Dookie!" I exclaimed while they already were frantically searching for our little friend.

Begonia pushed the ground cover away like a swimmer. I poked around the little lighted gnome homes and looked behind the gurgling fountain. Juniper was on her hands and knees, hoping to be more on his level. I ran over the little bridge to see if maybe he fell into the water. Could Dookie float? I had never tested to see if he was a good swimmer.

I started to get nervous when too much time had passed and we still hadn't found him. I would not leave this garden without taking my Dookie. I became so focused on finding my hamster that when the peacocks began to cry out, I almost didn't pay any attention to them. Begonia, who was not used to their cries, became distracted and noticed the birds weren't crying out for fun; something was scaring them. They seemed to be running in circles, trying to get away from something. Lucky for me, she saw Dookie scrambling along the ground, inadvertently intimidating the much larger creatures.

"There he is! There's Dookie," she called out.

I ran and grabbed him.

"And there you are …" a familiar, old, raspy voice said, creepier than usual as more thunder announced an oncoming storm.

I stood stone still. I knew this voice all too well. I had heard it yelling at us as we tried to escape from the stable house. The hidden messages between his words always spoke warnings of distrust. I knew the voice wasn't Major Whoopins' or Mr. Ree's … or Dookie's. It had to be that mean old fart, Mr. Meanor, whose voice sent a paralyzing chill through my bones. I was frozen. I could tell from Begonia's expression, if I turned around, I might be tormented by nightmares brought on by his intimidating face, forever.

"Where's yer friend?"

I willed myself to face him, and gained the courage to speak. "She's right there." I pointed to Begonia.

Without even a glance over to Begonia, he said, "Yer other friend."

"I have more than one friend. Could you be more specific?"

Mr. Meanor didn't like being told what to do by a little brat like me. He raised his voice, indicating his seriousness: "Oats."

"Oats? Oh, you mean Coriander?" I thought about it and wondered where Coriander could possibly be. "I don't know."

"Dab-nabbit, I see how this is going. I was trying to be … how do I say … uh… *nice* … but it seems you want to play games. I don't play games. And since you can't seem to stay put, maybe we can find someplace more suitable—I mean secure," he said in a tone suggesting bad things.

"Mr. Ree, help me escort these here snoopin' scoundrels to the hanging cage."

I hadn't even noticed Mr. Ree until now. The two men grabbed us and led us to the other side of the house. We trudged along reluctantly while I was secretly planning our escape. In the far distance, carried by a west wind, I heard a train whistle. I tried to shake off Mr. Ree's grip, but he had some crazy kung fu grip that sent a bolt of electricity through my body if I went even a little out of line.

CHAPTER 50

THE APPROACHING STORM

The moonlight cast a watchful glow onto the cage, which hung empty and waiting for children to torment, as troops of clouds invaded the night sky. The stillness I'd felt earlier must have been the calm before the storm. The thunder in the distance now came closer and grew louder. Mr. Ree pulled on the rope, letting out the pulley system which raised and lowered the cage. The cage rocked cockily toward the ground, sure of its task. Mean old Mr. Meanor pulled out his giant circle of skeleton keys, searching for the right one, while I sarcastically thought to myself about the hairpin I had given Coriander to open it when he was trapped within the hanging cage last time I was here.

"Flippin', flarmin', scootin', pootin', raspin' … darn danglin' keys," Mr. Meanor mumbled, and various other unintelligible words emerged while he fumbled with his keys, before he finally found the correct one to open the lock.

He tested the key and unlocked the door, and then pushed us in a little harder than necessary.

What if Dookie fell or something? I saw Begonia guarding Dookie steadfastly. She held him with a firm grip, under her shirt, by her belly.

Slowly, they raised the cylindrical cage … until they stopped and perched us under the branch of a strong oak tree. The men stood there for awhile watching us, to make sure we couldn't shake ourselves loose. Then they turned to go as the sky lit with a dazzling flash of lightning.

With the rumble of thunder echoing around us, despair began to set in. I didn't want this to be the way Begonia was greeted by The Children's Horrible House. She probably hated this place. I wasn't sure why I didn't. Even though The Children's Horrible House was gravely intimidating and spooky, it held a strange charm. But now that I was suffering in this cage, I came to agree: this house *was* horrible. The lightning flashed more and more frequently, and I was pretty sure, being in a metal cage under a tall oak tree, we were sitting ducks waiting to be electrocuted.

CHAPTER 51

FINDING JUNIPER

"Find Mr. Oats, now!" Director Pankins instructed her entire staff.

Major Whoopins, mean old Mr. Meanor, and Mr. Ree teamed up and scoured the rooms and hallways of The Children's Horrible House. The men made all the kids get out of bed and stand aside as they ripped the beds apart and made big messes that the kids had to clean up in their wake … like an invasion of the cleanliness once painfully achieved, only to be forced to repeat.

Déjeuner was extremely nervous, being all alone in her room while all this took place. The approaching storm outside didn't help, either. She hadn't been with Juniper since before dinner. Something felt strange and she had no idea what it could be. After the attack on her room and bed, she decided to search for Juniper.

In the wake of putting her bunk back together, Déjeuner tiptoed her way to the door. As she was feeling her way around, someone lurked behind her, and Déjeuner quickly turned.

"Hey … Déjeuner, it's me, Clovah. … I'm Holly's friend, rememba?"

Déjeuner pondered for moment, with her fingers brushing her chin. "Holly?"

"Yeah, Junipa's sistah."

"Oh. Yeah, I remember. You know where Juniper is?"

"No, but I have a feeling somethin' bad is about to happen. We need to find hah, now. Come with me."

Déjeuner took Clover's arm and they quickly and quietly searched the house. Without warning, a clap of thunder shook the entire house to its core. The two girls were thrown back by the strength of the rumbling. Pieces of the walls crumbled and hit the floor, causing an unbearable dust cloud. The girls coughed and sputtered, trying to breathe. Clover dusted herself off and grabbed Déjeuner's hand and led her out of the mess.

Carefully, they walked to the first door they could find to get out of the house that was shaking uncontrollably from the blasts of lightning and thunder. The weather was really serious. This storm was not messing around. Unsure of where to find the safest place to hide, they still decided locating Juniper was more important than their personal safety. All at once, the kids poured out of their rooms and the hallways turned into chaos. It was every kid for himself or herself.

CHAPTER 52

THE FURIOUS FIRE

As Begonia, Juniper, Dookie, and I hung like a piñata waiting for lightning to strike us and split us open, kids spewed out from all the doors of The Children's Horrible House. I had never seen so much chaos. Kids screamed and cried for their mommies, and the staff did little to help. I looked around, trying to find Clover and the PP twins. Most of the kids were strangers to me, except for the two ugliest girls in the world, Thistle and Nettle. I spotted them trampling over smaller kids trying to escape.

Juniper was alarmingly anxious, like she was looking for someone in particular, too.

"Oh, no! Where is she?"

"Who?" I asked.

"My sweet little Lunch."

"Who?" I was confused. Now was not the time to talk about food, plus it wasn't time for lunch. In fact, my stomach grumbled that it was way past dinnertime.

"Déjeuner."

"Déj-a-who?" Was she speaking in one of her accents? I was completely confused … and then lightning struck and the blasting booms that cracked were …

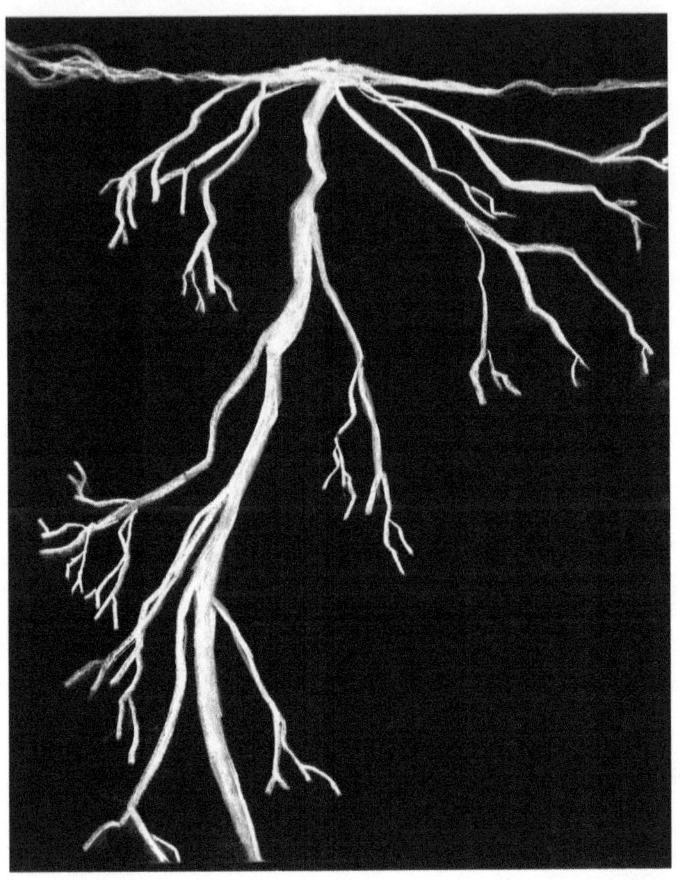

… deafening.

I was still alive … and so was everyone else; death had never felt so close. I could smell it. I could sense a terrible burning. It smelled like smoke—it was smoke. Something was on fire. Something big was on fire! Was The Children's Horrible House on fire? Oh, no! I was scared and this time, legitimately—not my overactive imagination. The three of us screamed and shook the cage, trying to get anyone's attention. But everyone was too worried for themselves.

A whistle blew, and the kids slowly settled after Major Whoopins yelled for them to settle down. Through a ringing bullhorn, he instructed them to form a line and follow him. Mr. Ree and Mr. Meanor corralled the kids who had a hard time listening to instructions.

"What about us?" I screamed, and the kids turned and looked up.

Major Whoopins instructed Mr. Meanor to let us out. The men led the kids away in the direction of the stable house, as Mr. Meanor hastily let the rope out while we dangled to the ground. As we were being lowered, I instructed Juniper and Begonia to follow my lead. I had a plan and it did not include being jerked around by mean old Mr. Meanor.

"You have a firm grip on Dookie?" I asked.

"Yes," Begonia replied.

"When I say go, you run as fast as you can to those woods," I whispered to them both, and they nodded.

Finally, the cage sat on solid ground. Mr. Meanor fumbled for his keys as large plops of rain dripped in slow motion around us. His hands shook as he frantically searched for the right key. The last bolt of lightning must have shaken him as well. He tried about six keys before he finally found the correct one.

As soon as the door clicked open, I rushed him and, with the door, knocked him over. "Go!" I said, and the three of us ran for our lives.

We made it to the woods and hid behind a thicket of bushes. Mr. Meanor didn't know what hit him. He took a long time to get up. As the rain grew heavier it must have made him come to consciousness. We could see him fumble and stumble his way toward the stable house. The backside of The Children's Horrible House was strangely lit with a warm glow. It dawned on me … what I saw was the fire I had smelled earlier.

Oh, no ….

I ran through the woods without looking back. Thankfully, Juniper and Begonia followed me. I ran until I tripped over a large weird lump.

"Ouch!" a voice cried out from the ground.

"Huh?" I rubbed my head, trying to figure out what made me stumble, when I saw Coriander come out of the ground like a dead body. A scream escaped my mouth before Juniper grabbed me and muted my overreaction. I pulled her hand away when I caught hold of my voice.

"Coriander! Where have you been?"

"I've been hiding ever since the garden caught fire."

"The garden? The glowing garden? Nooooo!"

I looked toward the flames and saw the garden engulfed. Through the angry blaze, I spotted the once green trickling leaves of the weeping willow being torched in torment. I started to run toward the willow as if I could rescue the tree, when Coriander pulled me back. My worst fears were coming true! I felt like I had seen this before, like déjà vu. Then it came back to me instantly—the dream I had when I had been here last. I *had* seen this before.

"Holly! No. You can't do anything except possibly get very hurt," Coriander told me in a stern voice.

"But …." I pointed, without being able to find the words to describe the hurt I felt, watching the beautiful night-blooming garden ablaze. The fire was ferocious, like a monster with a purpose—to destroy what was once the most peaceful, most tranquil, beyond beautiful place to not only reflect and heal, but also to rest. Hawthorne North Star's mausoleum wasn't even visible from this point.

"I know, I know," Coriander said. "There is nothing we can do except hope the rain can put out the flames before it catches the whole house and the entire estate on fire." He was offering the only solution that could possibly put out the flames besides an entire troop of firetrucks filled with firemen.

I said, "What about Clover, Staniel, and Danley? We have to make sure they get out of the house before the house burns down!"

"And Déjeuner too!" Juniper said.

Who? I wondered, but didn't have time to question her.

"Coriander, we have to find our friends. I could never live with myself if something bad happened to them."

"How do you know they are even here?" he asked.

Juniper said, "They're here. I've met Clover, and those twins are hard to miss."

"I understand, but we might get hurt or even killed trying."

"Coriander, we have to, we just have to."

"Let's go! Let's save them," Begonia said, even though she didn't know a single one of these people.

That was all the pep talk we needed. Without any more hesitation, we ran to The Children's Horrible House.

CHAPTER 53

SLAMMED SHUT

Clover and Déjeuner stood inside near the front door, and watched all the kids funnel out of the doors, afraid of the stampede, and the waves of wind and rain. As the two waited for the crowds to dissipate, without warning, four hands came from behind Clover and covered her eyes.

She put her hands over them and turned around with a smile. "Can't fool me, guys." Clover smirked at the twins.

"We thought if we covered only your good eye, you might think we were Holly."

"Stop it," Clover playfully said.

"We should probably get out of here," Déjeuner said, noting the empty hallway.

In a wink, the main door they had been looking out from slammed shut, either from the violent storm wreaking havoc outside, or someone being inconsiderate.

"Oh, no," Déjeuner cried out while pulling on the door handle.

"It's okay, we'll open it back up," Staniel said as the twins stalked over to open the door—it would not open. "What's going on? Why won't it open?"

"It must be jammed," Danley pointed out.

A blast of thunder shook the house so violently, something crashed in another part of the house. The oil-lit fixtures snuffed out and darkness consumed the rooms around them.

Déjeuner clung to Clover and Clover held her close. The twins tried to act brave; however, their frightened eyes gave their fears away. From the main hall, the subtle sounds of tic and tac, tic and tac, came closer. The pace sounded familiar. It became obvious the steps belonged to Miss Judge, who casually walked as if there wasn't a terrifying storm outside trapping them inside an enormous, frightening house.

"Well, hello," she said, evidently surprised to see the huddled children.

"Hello, Miss Judge," they all responded.

"Are you going to the stable house?"

Clover said, "We're stuck. The door is jammed."

She tromped over and shook it, banged on it, and followed that with a kick, before she turned to them and said, "It's definitely stuck. Let's find another exit."

CHAPTER 54

HONOR, TRUST, AND VICTIMS

Sirius gathered her most valued possessions for fear they might not be found after the violent storm finished its rampage.

As a flash of lightning struck another object in the near distance, her office door rudely opened without even a knock, and a low, brusque voice spoke: "I thought I could trust you. I should have known better."

All she could see was a shadow filling the space in the doorway. For a second she thought it could be her father and she became excited and frightened at once … until another menacing flash of lightning illuminated the lined face of Reed Trustworthy, and she dropped everything she held.

Though frightened, Sirius tried to regain her composure. She picked up her things and said, "I thought I could trust a lot of people. Sadly, that was a lesson learned the hard way."

"Don't act like such a victim," he said. "Your own actions have led to your unhappiness."

"I suppose you believe I drove my mother away when I was eight?"

"Not when you were eight, no."

Sirius was confused. What could he mean by this? "I never wanted my mother to leave."

Reed said, "Then why couldn't you at least honor her? Instead you wasted all the things she gave to you in those years when she was here. I saw her pour immeasurable good into you. Then you squandered her teachings away and turned her legacy into a spoiled, rotten brat—which drove your father to his grave."

The words stung, and Sirius had no rebuttal. If it weren't for the chair poised beneath her, she would have crumpled to the ground. Her tears and sobs were muffled by the outside raindrops.

Reed stepped into the office and said, "I'm not falling for this … again."

"I'm not crying for you."

"Who, then? Let me guess. Your mother and father, I suppose."

"No." She sniffed. "I'm crying for me."

"That's not surprising. It should have been my first guess, considering how selfish you are."

"You will never understand."

"I can't argue with things I agree with."

"Reed, what are you doing here? Are you here to torment me? To make sure I stay miserable?"

"No," he said, stepping closer and standing next to her desk. "I'm here to help, actually. I'm just not sure who to help, yet."

"What do you mean?"

"It's between you … and … your sister."

Sirius looked around at nothing in particular, trying to understand his meaning, and said, "I'm not sure what you mean."

"I think you do."

CHAPTER 55

IT WILL BE MESSY

Leaves swirled clockwise and lifted into a funnel, and then spewed about in every direction. As I ran to the house, a large sycamore leaf landed right in the middle of my face like a mask, temporarily blinding me. I grabbed it off and threw it aside. At the main entrance, the door stayed substantially shut. Juniper grabbed the iron knocker and pounded on the door; it seemed to make no sound. Coriander tried pushing the door open by slamming his shoulders into it … one, and then the other. He was no match for the solidity of this monstrous threshold. His efforts were useless; if Coriander couldn't open it, there was little to no chance for me to succeed.

I tried to think of a way I could get in and remembered the door in the back near the garden. It might be too dangerous, being so close to the fire. Then I remembered THE DUNGEON and how I once escaped from it. I knew we could get through there; however, it would be messy.

"How are we going to get in?" Juniper asked, while the wild weather pulled her hair around like marionettes. "We can't open this door, and the back door is probably blocked off by flames. Holly, I'm not sure they are even in here. What if they're in the stable house with all the other kids?"

"Why don't you and Begonia go look for them at the stable house while Coriander and I search for them in here," I said.

Begonia asked, "How will we know if you found them or not?"

"We'll come to the stable house if or when we find them," I practically yelled, thanks to the loud storm. "So make sure you stay there, even if they're not there, okay?"

"Okay." Juniper wrapped her arms around Begonia, protecting her from the rain, and they staggered into the darkness.

Coriander asked, "What's the plan?"

"THE DUNGEON," I replied.

"I think it's too close to the fire."

"It's far enough away, I think. But we must hurry. Let's go."

When we arrived at the manure spreader, I knew we were right outside the wall of THE DUNGEON. The storm blurred my vision. The rain dwindled, but the wind was still vicious. I grabbed the shovel from the spreader and started digging under the wall. Quickly, I ran out of steam and my hands felt raw. Coriander grabbed the shovel and took over. Boy, did he make my efforts look silly. I told myself I probably made it easier on him because I had already dug this out once before. I could see a sliver of light appear from the other side of the ditch. I kneeled and, with my hands, moved globs of dirt out of the way. Coriander used the shovel to make a nice tunnel for us to get through. He stabbed the shovel into the ground, indicating that he had finished. We crawled under the wall, into THE DUNGEON.

CHAPTER 56

NOTHING TO LOSE

Miss Judge led the children to the back lower door, down the stairs from her library. As they walked, Déjeuner hummed while holding tightly to Clover's arm. Clover petted her hand, reassuring Déjeuner of her safety. Since these ladies walked so excruciatingly slow, Staniel's and Danley's feet scuffed the floors as they followed. Miss Judge's high-heeled Mary Janes tipped and tapped on the floors in some sort of rhythm that could put some people under hypnosis.

They began descending the stairs, when Déjeuner gasped and said, "We can't go out this way."

"Why?" asked Clover.

"It's too dangerous. … I can feel the heat; something is on fire."

"Is it the house?" Miss Judge asked while sniffing the air, which now, more than before, suggested smoke.

"I'm not sure. I feel it out there." Déjeuner pointed at the door.

Miss Judge put her hand on the door and immediately pulled it away. "She's right. Something is on fire. I hope it's not the house." Miss Judge's face became worried. "I have to get Copper, before something happens to him." Miss Judge turned to go back up the stairs, toward her library.

"What about us?" Clover asked.

"Wait here, I'll be right back." Miss Judge ran up and away.

After only a brief pause, Staniel said, "I'm not waiting here to get burned to a charred piece of meat. I think we need to find another way out."

He and Danley grabbed both girls' arms and started walking up the stairs. At the landing, they weren't sure where to go next as another big blast of thunder shook the house.

Clover said, "I nevah thought I'd say this evah … but I think … the safest place for us … right now … is THE DUNGEON."

"THE DUNGEON?" Déjeuner didn't seem to like the sound of this idea.

Staniel said, "You know, you're probably right. Holly was able to dig her way out of there before. It wouldn't hurt to go check."

"It could hurt, if someone like Major Whoopins or Director Pankins is there waiting to paddle someone," Déjeuner said.

"I doubt, with all this going on and all the other kids being taken to the stable house, Director Pankins and Major Whoopins are looking to spank anyone," Danley said.

"At this point, we have nothing to lose," Staniel decided.

"Nothing except the feeling in our butts if we get caught," Déjeuner said.

"Trust us," Staniel said. "Plus, we aren't technically doing anything wrong. So why would we get spankings?"

Déjeuner cocked her head to the side as she thought briefly. "I guess you're right. Let's go."

The four of them quickly ran through the hallways, toward the stairs leading them to THE DUNGEON. As their feet hit each step, it seemed like they became more implanted into the actual being of the house. A feeling of fright overcame them, even though they thought they were headed in the right direction. The earthen-bricked walls began to enclose around them as they stepped deeper and deeper. Only one dimly lit flame provided a little illumination. They could hardly see in front of them when they came to the heavy iron door. From within, they heard some faint noises. Was someone inside?

Clover put her ear to the door. "Maybe this wasn't such a good idea," Clover whispered.

CHAPTER 57

THE DUNGEON WORMS

Like worms, we inched our way through the tunnel and under the wall of the dark, dank, moldy-smelling dungeon.

"Ugh, ugh, eegh, humph, pumph."

"SHHHHHH!" Coriander shushed me for being too dramatic with my crawling noises.

While breathing, I accidentally took some dirt into my mouth and spat it out. Unfortunately, I then had to crawl through my own spit. *Eww.* I could still taste the brown remnants of earth and forced myself to go farther, despite my discomfort. Finally, I made it. I stood and wiped off the loose mud and dirt. There was no light except for the bits peeking through the hinges of the door. Thankfully, Coriander was right behind me and he too wiped off his clothes before deciding what to do next.

"It's hard to see," he said.

"It is, yes. At least we're in." I felt triumphant, and opened the door from the small room off the main chamber of THE DUNGEON.

"Yes, we are, but how do you suppose we open that very large, most-likely locked, door?" Coriander said, pointing to the massive iron aperture which required a key to open.

"Oops," I said.

"That's all you're going to say? Oops?"

"Do you have something better to say?"

"Darn."

"That's not better. It's only different from what I said."

"No, I mean *darn*, like *darn it*, what are we going to do now?"

"Oh."

Coriander looked around, trying to find something—a key, probably. The likeliness of finding the right one would be next to nothing.

Without even thinking, I said, "Maybe we should knock." I put my knuckles to the door and knocked five times, the way my brothers and sisters used to always do it … *Knock-knock-knock-knock-knock* … (*Shave and a Haircut*).

CHAPTER 58

SHAVE AND A HAIRCUT

"Did you hear that?" Clover lifted her head from the door. "That was *Shave and a Haircut.*"

Déjeuner said, "Oh, I heard it, all right. Who do you think is in there?"

"I have no idea," Staniel said, "but there's only one way to find out."

Staniel said, "What if it's—"

Danley said, "I highly doubt it's Director Pankins or Major Whoopins. They have a key, first of all. And second, well … I don't have a second reason." He stopped trying to prove his point.

With no more hesitation, Déjeuner exclaimed, "Answer back!"

Clover put her hand to the door and answered with two rhythmic knocks: *Two bits.*

CHAPTER 59

TWO BITS

After hearing little to nothing for a while after I knocked, I was stunned to hear the two answering raps come from the other side of the door. Coriander stopped searching and crossed over to the door, beside me.

"Knock again," he said.

Knock-knock-knock-knock-knock, my fist delivered to the person on the other side of the door. Faster this time, we were answered with two quick beats.

"Who's there?" asked the unmistakable raspy voices of Staniel and Danley.

My eyes grew wide, and I could have leaped a thousand feet in the air if the ten-foot ceilings didn't block my ascension.

"It's us, Holly and Coriander!"

"Holly? Corianda?" Clover's deep voice and unique accent sliced through the door, to my ears.

"Clover!" I could hardly contain myself.

"I'm here too."

I heard a sweet-sounding voice I was unfamiliar with. I tried to place the voice with a face, but couldn't make a match.

"Hi, whoever you are!" I said so excited I could greet even perfect strangers.

Then I heard nothing, only the static of white noise that fills emptiness.

"Hello?" I called.

Nothing.

"Hello? Clover? Staniel, Danley? Are you there? It's me, Holly and Coriander."

Nothing.

I knocked the five secret code raps quickly.

Abruptly the door lock opened, and my smile spread from ear to ear. I was ready to give each of them a big fat hug—and then my smile vanished.

"*Two bits,*" Director Sirius Pankins slowly and dreadfully sang.

BE ON THE LOOKOUT FOR:

ESCAPE FROM THE CHILDREN'S HORRIBLE HOUSE

The director's lips spread to a wide, menacing smile. What was in between her teeth to the left of her canine? Spinach? Again? I stared at her mouth, and then her lips smacked shut.

"What are you looking at?" she snapped.

I shook my head, not wanting to antagonize her further.

"Speak!" she commanded.

"Nothing, ma'am. Just surprised to see you, that's all."

"Surprised, I'm sure …."

About the Author

N. Jane Quackenbush is a graduate of Palm Beach Atlantic University. She lives in a horrible house filled with mystery and fun in St. Augustine, Florida, a place she finds a lot of material by which she is inspired. A lot of the places mentioned in this book are based on actual haunted buildings, star-filled planetariums and magical gardens deep within The Nation's Oldest City. If you can find and name them, please let Ms. Quackenbush know by contacting her at www.hiddenwolfbooks.com.

You can also stay in touch with N. Jane Quackenbush on Facebook.

N. Jane Quackenbush has also written the following Children's Picture Books:

The Rocket Ship Bed Trip
The Pirate Ship Bed Trip
The Afternoon Moon
Light on Darkness Lies
The Children's Horrible House
and many more in the works!

If you enjoyed reading *Return to The Children's Horrible House*, please leave a review.

Watch the trailer on You Tube:
https://youtu.be/hXoZ0XXCyKQ

www.ingramcontent.com/pod-product-compliance
Lightning Source LLC
Chambersburg PA
CBHW031957040826
48979CB00042B/499
9780996892209